Jonathan Edwards
Selected Sermons of Jonathan Edwards

Jonathan Edwards
Selected Sermons of Jonathan Edwards

Selected Sermons of

Jonathan Edwards

By Jonathan Edwards

CONTENTS

GOD GLORIFIED IN MAN'S DEPENDENCE°

1 COR. i. 29-31.—That no flesh should glory in his presence. But of him are ye in Christ Jesus, who of God is made unto us wisdom, and righteousness, and sanctification, and redemption: that according as it is written, He that glorieth, let him glory in the Lord.

Those Christians to whom the apostle directed this epistle dwelt in a part of the world where human wisdom was in great repute; as the apostle observes in the 22d verse of this chapter, "The Greeks seek after wisdom." Corinth was not far from Athens, that had been for many ages the most famous seat of philosophy and learning in the world.

The apostle therefore observes to them how that God, by the gospel, destroyed and brought to nought their human wisdom. The learned Grecians and their great philosophers by all their wisdom did not know God: they were not able to find out the truth in divine things. But after they had done their utmost to no effect, it pleased God at length to reveal himself by the gospel, which they accounted foolishness. He "chose the foolish things of the world to confound the wise, and the weak things of the world to confound the things which are mighty, and the base things of the world, and things that are despised, yea, and things which are not, to bring to nought the things that are." And the apostle informs them why he thus did, in the verse of the text: *That no flesh should glory in his presence*, &c.

In which words may be observed,

1. What God aims at in the disposition of things in the affair of redemption, viz., that man should not glory in himself, but alone in God: *That no flesh should glory in his presence,—that, according as it is written, He that glorieth, let him glory in the Lord.*

2. How this end is attained in the work of redemption, viz., by that absolute and immediate dependence which men have upon God in that work for all their good. Inasmuch as,

First, All the good that they have is in and through Christ; *he is made unto us wisdom, righteousness, sanctification, and redemption.* All the good of the fallen and redeemed creature is concerned in these four things, and cannot be better distributed than into them; but Christ is each of them to us, and we have none of them any otherwise than in him. *He is made of God unto us wisdom:* in him are all the proper good and true excellency of the understanding. Wisdom was a thing that the Greeks admired; but Christ is the true light of the world, it is through him alone that true wisdom is imparted to the mind. 'Tis in and by Christ that we have *righteousness:* it is by being in him that we are justified, have our sins pardoned, and are received as righteous into God's favor. 'Tis by Christ that we have *sanctification:* we have in him true excellency of heart as well as of understanding; and he is made unto us inherent, as well as imputed righteousness. 'Tis by Christ that we have *redemption,* or actual deliverance from all misery, and the bestowment of all happiness and glory. Thus we have all our good by Christ, who is God.

Secondly, Another instance wherein our dependence on God for all our good appears, is this, that it is God that has given us Christ, that we might have these benefits through him; he *of God is made unto us wisdom, righteousness*, &c.

Thirdly, 'Tis *of him* that we are in Christ Jesus, and come to have an interest in him, and so do receive those blessings which he is made unto us. It is God that gives us faith whereby we close with Christ.

So that in this verse is shown our dependence on each person in the Trinity for all our good. We are dependent on Christ the Son of God, as he is our wisdom, righteousness, sanctification and redemption. We are dependent on the Father, who has given us Christ, and made him to be these things to us. We are dependent on the Holy Ghost, for 'tis *of him that we are in Christ Jesus*; 'tis the Spirit of God that gives faith in him, whereby we receive him and close with him.

DOCTRINE

God is glorified in the work of redemption in this, that there appears in it so absolute and universal a dependence of the redeemed on him.

Here I propose to show, I., That there is an absolute and universal dependence of the redeemed on God for all their good. And II., That God hereby is exalted and glorified in the work of redemption.

I. There is an absolute and universal dependence of the redeemed on God. The nature and contrivance of our redemption is such, that the redeemed are in every thing directly, immediately and entirely dependent on God: they are dependent on him for all, and are dependent on him every way.

The several ways wherein the dependence of one being may be upon another for its good, and wherein the redeemed of Jesus Christ depend on God for all their good, are these, viz., that they have all their good *of* him, and that they have all *through* him, and that they have all *in* him. That he is the cause and original whence all their good comes, therein it is *of* him; and that he is the medium by which it is obtained and conveyed, therein they have it *through* him; and that he is that good itself that is given and conveyed, therein it is *in* him.

Now those that are redeemed by Jesus Christ do, in all these respects, very directly and entirely depend on God for their all.

First, The redeemed have all their good *of* God; God is the great author of it; he is the first cause of it, and not only so, but he is the only proper cause.

'Tis of God that we have our Redeemer: it is God that has provided a Saviour for us. Jesus Christ is not only of God in his person, as he is the only begotten Son of God, but he is from God, as we are concerned in him and in his office of Mediator: he is the gift of God to us: God chose and anointed him, appointed him his work, and sent him into the world.

And as it is God that gives, so 'tis God that accepts the Saviour. As it is God that provides and gives the Redeemer to buy salvation for us, so it is of God that salvation is bought: he gives the purchaser, and he affords the thing purchased.

'Tis of God that Christ becomes ours, that we are brought to him and are united to him: it is of God that we receive faith to close with him, that we may have an interest in him. Eph. ii. 8, "For by grace ye are saved, through faith; and that not of yourselves, it is the gift of God." 'Tis of God that we actually do receive all the benefits that Christ has purchased. 'Tis God that pardons and justifies, and delivers from going down to hell, and it is his favor that the redeemed are received into, and are made the objects of, when they are justified. So it is God that delivers from the dominion of sin, and cleanses us from our filthiness, and changes us from our deformity. It is of God that the redeemed do receive all their true excellency, wisdom and holiness; and that two ways, viz., as the Holy Ghost, by whom these things are immediately wrought, is from God, proceeds from him and is sent by him; and also as the Holy Ghost himself is God, by whose operation and indwelling the knowledge of divine things, and a holy disposition, and all grace, are conferred and upheld.

And though means are made use of in conferring grace on men's souls, yet 'tis of God that we have these means of grace, and 'tis God that makes them effectual. 'Tis of God that we have the holy Scriptures; they are the word of God. 'Tis of God that we have ordinances, and their efficacy depends on the immediate influence of the Spirit of God. The ministers of the gospel are sent of God, and all their sufficiency is of him. 2 Cor. iv. 7, "We have this treasure in earthen vessels, that the excellency of the power may be of God, and not of us." Their success depends entirely and absolutely on the immediate blessing and influence of God. The redeemed have all.

1. Of the *grace* of God. It was of mere grace that God gave us his only begotten Son. The grace is great in proportion to the dignity and excellency of what is given: the gift was infinitely precious, because it was a person infinitely worthy, a person of infinite glory; and also because it was a person infinitely near and dear to God. The grace is great in proportion to the benefit we have given us in him: the benefit is doubly infinite, in that in him we have deliverance from an infinite, because an eternal, misery; and do also receive eternal joy and glory. The grace in bestowing this gift is great in proportion to our unworthiness to whom it is given; instead of deserving such a gift, we merited infinitely ill of God's hands. The grace is great according to the manner of giving, or in proportion to the humiliation and expense of the method and means by which way is made for our having of the gift. He gave him to us dwelling amongst us; he gave him to us incarnate, or in our nature; he gave him to us in our nature, in the like infirmities in which we have it in our fallen state, and which in us do accompany and are occasioned by the sinful corruption of our nature. He gave him to us in a low and afflicted state; and not only so, but he gave him to us slain, that he might be a feast for our souls.°

The grace of God in bestowing this gift is most free. It was what God was under no obligation to bestow: he might have rejected fallen man, as he did the fallen angels. It was what we never did any thing to merit. 'Twas given while we were yet enemies, and before we had so much as repented. It was from the love of God that saw no excellency in us to attract it; and it was without expectation of ever being requited for it.

And 'tis from mere grace that the benefits of Christ are applied to such and such particular persons. Those that are called and sanctified are to attribute it alone to the good pleasure of God's goodness, by which they are distinguished. He is sovereign, and hath mercy on whom he will have mercy, and whom he will, he hardens.

Man hath now a greater dependence on the grace of God than he had before the fall. He depends on the free goodness of God for much more than he did then: then he depended on God's goodness for conferring the reward of perfect obedience: for God was not obliged to promise and bestow that reward: but now we are dependent on the grace of God for much more: we stand in need of grace, not only to bestow glory upon us, but to deliver us from hell and eternal wrath. Under the first covenant we depended on God's goodness to give us the reward of righteousness; and so we do now. And not only so, but we stand in need of God's free and sovereign grace to give us that righteousness; and yet not only so, but we stand in need of his grace to pardon our sin and release us from the guilt and infinite demerit of it.

And as we are dependent on the goodness of God for more now than under the first covenant, so we are dependent on a much greater, more free and wonderful goodness. We are now more dependent on God's arbitrary and sovereign good pleasure. We were in our first estate dependent on God for holiness: we had our original righteousness from him; but then holiness was not bestowed in such a way of sovereign good pleasure as it is now. Man was created holy, and it became God to create holy all the reasonable creatures he created: it would have been a disparagement to the holiness of God's nature, if he had made an intelligent creature unholy. But now when a man is made holy, it is from mere and arbitrary grace; God may forever deny holiness to the fallen creature if he pleases, without any disparagement to any of his perfections.

And we are not only indeed more dependent on the grace of God, but our dependence is much more conspicuous, because our own insufficiency and helplessness in ourselves is much more apparent in our fallen and undone state than it was before we were either sinful or miserable. We are more apparently dependent on God for holiness, because we are first sinful, and utterly polluted, and afterward holy: so the production of the effect is sensible, and its derivation from God more obvious. If man was ever holy and always was so, it would not be so apparent, that he had not holiness necessarily, as an inseparable qualification of human nature. So we are more apparently dependent on free grace for the favor of God, for we are first justly the objects of his displeasure and afterwards are received into favor. We are more apparently dependent on God for happiness, being first miserable and afterwards happy. It is more apparently free and without merit in us, because we are actually without any kind of excellency to merit, if there could be any such thing as merit in creature excellency. And we are not only without any true excellency, but are full of, and wholly defiled with, that which is infinitely odious. All our good is more apparently from God, because we are first naked and wholly without any good, and afterwards enriched with all good.

2. We receive all of the *power* of God. Man's redemption is often spoken of as a work of wonderful power as well as grace. The great power of God appears in bringing a sinner from his low state, from the depths of sin and misery, to such an exalted state of holiness and happiness. Eph. i. 19, "And what is the exceeding greatness of his power to usward who believe, according to the working of his mighty power."

We are dependent on God's power through every step of our redemption. We are dependent on the power of God to convert us, and give faith in Jesus Christ, and the new nature. 'Tis a work of creation: "If any man be in Christ, he is a new creature," 2 Cor. v. 17. "We are created in Christ Jesus," Eph. ii. 10. The fallen creature cannot attain to true holiness, but by being created again: Eph. iv. 24, "And that ye put on the new man, which after God is created in righteousness and true holiness." It is a raising from the dead: Col ii. 12, 13, "Wherein ye also are risen with him, through the faith of the operation of God, who hath raised him from the dead." Yea, it is a more glorious work of power than mere creation, or raising a dead body to life, in that the effect attained is greater and more excellent. That holy and happy being and spiritual life which is reached in the work of conversion is a far greater and more glorious effect than mere being and life. And the state from whence the change is made, of such a death in sin, and total corruption of nature, and depth of misery, is far more remote from the state attained, than mere death or nonentity.

'Tis by God's power also that we are preserved in a state of grace: 1 Pet. i. 5, "Who are kept by the power of God through faith unto salvation." As grace is at first from God, so 'tis continually from him, and is maintained by him, as much as light in the atmosphere is all day long from the sun, as well as at first dawning or at sunrising.

Men are dependent on the power of God for every exercise of grace, and for carrying on the work of grace in the heart, for the subduing of sin and corruption, and increasing holy principles, and enabling to bring forth fruit in good works, and at last bringing grace to its perfection, in making the soul completely amiable in Christ's glorious likeness, and filling of it with a satisfying joy and blessedness; and for the raising of the body to life, and to such a perfect state, that it shall be suitable for a habitation and organ for a soul so perfected and blessed. These are the most glorious effects of the power of God that are seen in the series of God's acts with respect to the creatures.

Man was dependent on the power of God in his first estate, but he is more dependent on his power now; he needs God's power to do more things for him, and depends on a more wonderful exercise of his power. It was an effect of the power of God to make man holy at the first; but more remarkably so now, because there is a great deal of opposition and difficulty in the way. 'Tis a more glorious effect of power to make that holy that was so depraved and under the dominion of sin, than to confer holiness on that which before had nothing of the contrary. It is a more glorious work of power to rescue a soul out of the hands of the devil, and from the powers of darkness, and to bring it into a state of salvation, than to confer holiness where there was no prepossession or opposition. Luke xi. 21, 22, "When a strong man armed keepeth his palace, his goods are in peace; but when a stronger than he shall come upon him, and overcome him, he taketh from him all his armor wherein he trusted, and divideth his spoils." So 'tis a more glorious work of power to uphold a soul in a state of grace and holiness, and to carry it on till it is brought to glory, when there is so much sin remaining in the heart resisting, and Satan with all his might opposing, than it would have been to have kept man from falling at first, when Satan had nothing in man.

Thus we have shown how the redeemed are dependent on God for all their good, as they have all *of* him.

Secondly, They are also dependent on God for all, as they have all *through* him. 'Tis God that is the medium of it, as well as the author and fountain of it. All that we have, wisdom and the pardon of sin, deliverance from hell, acceptance in God's favor, grace and holiness, true comfort and happiness, eternal life and glory, we have from God by a Mediator; and this Mediator is God, which Mediator we have an absolute dependence upon as he *through* whom we receive all. So that here is another way wherein we have our dependence on God for all good. God not only gives us the Mediator, and accepts his mediation, and of his power and grace bestows the things purchased by the Mediator, but he is the Mediator.

Our blessings are what we have by purchase; and the purchase is made of God, the blessings are purchased of him, and God gives the purchaser; and not only so, but God is the purchaser. Yea, God is both the purchaser and the price; for Christ, who is God, purchased these blessings for us by offering up himself as the price of our salvation. He purchased eternal life by the sacrifice of himself: Heb. vii. 27, "He offered up himself;" and ix. 26, "He hath appeared to take away sin by the sacrifice of himself." Indeed it was the human nature that was offered; but it was the same person with the divine, and therefore was an infinite price: it was looked upon as if God had been offered in sacrifice.

As we thus have our good through God, we have a dependence on God in a respect that man in his first estate had not. Man was to have eternal life then through his own righteousness; so that he had partly a dependence upon what was in himself; for we have a dependence upon that through which we have our good, as well as that from which we have it. And though man's righteousness that he then depended on was indeed from God, yet it was his own, it was inherent in himself; so that his dependence was not so immediately on God. But now the righteousness that we are dependent on is not in ourselves, but in God. We are saved through the righteousness of Christ: he *is made unto us righteousness*, and therefore is prophesied of, Jer. xxiii. 6, under that name of "the Lord our righteousness." In that the righteousness we are justified by is the righteousness of Christ, it is the righteousness of God: 2 Cor. v. 21, "That we might be made the righteousness of God in him."

Thus in redemption we han't only all things of God, but by and through him: 1 Cor. viii. 21, "But to us there is but one God, the Father, of whom are all things, and we in him; and one Lord Jesus Christ, by whom are all things, and we by him."

Thirdly, The redeemed have all their good *in* God. We not only have it of him, and through him, but it consists in him; he *is* all our good.

The good of the redeemed is either objective or inherent. By their objective good I mean that intrinsic object, in the possession and enjoyment of which they are happy. Their inherent good is that excellency or pleasure which is in the soul itself. With respect to both of which the redeemed have all their good in God, or, which is the same thing, God himself is all their good.

1. The redeemed have all their *objective* good in God. God himself is the great good which they are brought to the possession and enjoyment of by redemption. He is the highest good and the sum of all that good which Christ purchased. God is the inheritance of the saints; he is the portion of their souls. God is their wealth and treasure, their food, their life, their dwelling-place, their ornament and diadem, and their everlasting honor and glory. They have none in heaven but God; he is the great good which the redeemed are received to at death, and which they are to rise to at the end of the world. The Lord God, he is the light of the heavenly Jerusalem; and is the "river of the water of life," that runs, and "the tree of life that grows, in the midst of the paradise of God." The glorious excellencies and beauty of God will be what will forever entertain the minds of the saints, and the love of God will be their everlasting feast. The redeemed will indeed enjoy other things; they will enjoy the angels, and will enjoy one another; but that which they shall enjoy in the angels, or each

other, or in any thing else whatsoever that will yield them delight and happiness, will be what will be seen of God in them.

2. The redeemed have all their *inherent* good in God. Inherent good is twofold; 'tis either excellency or pleasure. These the redeemed not only derive from God, as caused by him, but have them in him. They have spiritual excellency and joy by a kind of participation of God. They are made excellent by a communication of God's excellency: God puts his own beauty, i.e., his beautiful likeness, upon their souls: they are made partakers of the divine nature, or moral image of God, 2 Pet. i. 4. They are holy by being made partakers of God's holiness, Heb. xii. 10. The saints are beautiful and blessed by a communication of God's holiness and joy, as the moon and planets are bright by the sun's light. The saint hath spiritual joy and pleasure by a kind of effusion of God on the soul. In these things the redeemed have communion with God; that is, they partake with him and of him.

The saints have both their spiritual excellency and blessedness by the gift of the Holy Ghost, or Spirit of God, and his dwelling in them. They are not only caused by the Holy Ghost, but are in the Holy Ghost as their principle. The Holy Spirit becoming an inhabitant, is a vital principle in the soul: he, acting in, upon and with the soul, becomes a fountain of true holiness and joy, as a spring is of water, by the exertion and diffusion of itself: John iv. 14, "But whosoever drinketh of the water that I shall give him, shall never thirst; but the water that I shall give him, shall be in him a well of water springing up into everlasting life,"—compared with chap. vii. 38, 39, "He that believeth on me, as the Scripture hath said, out of his belly shall flow rivers of living water; but this spake he of the Spirit, which they that believe on him should receive." The sum of what Christ has purchased for us is that spring of water spoken of in the former of those places, and those rivers of living water spoken of in the latter. And the sum of the blessings which the redeemed shall receive in heaven is that river of water of life that proceeds from the throne of God and the Lamb, Rev. xxii. 1,—which doubtless signifies the same with those rivers of living water explained John vii. 38, 39, which is elsewhere called the "river of God's pleasures." Herein consists the fulness of good which the saints receive by Christ. 'Tis by partaking of the Holy Spirit that they have communion with Christ in his fulness. God hath given the Spirit, not by measure unto him, and they do receive of his fulness, and grace for grace. This is the sum of the saints' inheritance; and therefore that little of the Holy Ghost which believers have in this world is said to be the earnest of their inheritance. 2 Cor. i. 22, "Who hath also sealed us, and given us the Spirit in our hearts." And chap. v. 5, "Now he that hath wrought us for the selfsame thing is God, who also hath given unto us the earnest of the Spirit." And Eph. i. 13, 14, "Ye were sealed with that Holy Spirit of promise, which is the earnest of our inheritance, until the redemption of the purchased possession."

The Holy Spirit and good things are spoken of in Scripture as the same; as if the Spirit of God communicated to the soul comprised all good things: Matt. vii. 11, "How much more shall your heavenly Father give good things to them that ask him?" In Luke it is, chap. xi. 13, "How much more shall your heavenly Father give the Holy Spirit to them that ask him?" This is the sum of the blessings that Christ died to procure, and that are the subject of gospel promises: Gal. iii. 13, 14, "He was made a curse for us, that we might receive the promise of the Spirit through faith." The Spirit of God is the great promise of the Father: Luke xxiv. 49, "Behold, I send the promise of my Father upon you." The Spirit of God therefore is called "the Spirit of promise," Eph. i. 13. This promised thing Christ received, and had given into his hand, as soon as he had finished the work of our redemption, to bestow on all that he had redeemed: Acts ii. 33, "Therefore, being by the right hand of God exalted, and having received of the Father the promise of the Holy Ghost, he hath shed forth this, which ye both see and hear." So that all the holiness and happiness of the redeemed is *in* God. 'Tis in the communications, indwelling and acting of the Spirit of God. Holiness and happiness are in the fruit, here and hereafter, because God dwells in them, and they in God.

Thus 'tis God that has given us the Redeemer, and 'tis of him that our good is purchased: so 'tis God that is the Redeemer and the price; and 'tis God also that is the good purchased. So that all that we have is *of* God, and *through* him, and *in* him: Rom. xi. 36, "For of him, and through him, and to him (or in him), are all things." The same in the Greek that is here rendered *to him* is rendered *in him*, I Cor. vii. 6.

II. God is glorified in the work of redemption by this means, viz., by there being so great and universal a dependence of the redeemed on him.

I. Man hath so much the greater occasion and obligation to take notice and acknowledge God's perfections and all-sufficiency. The greater the creature's dependence is on God's perfections, and the greater concern he has with them, so much the greater occasion has he to take notice of them. So much the greater concern any one has with, and dependence upon, the power and grace of God, so much the greater occasion has he to take notice of that power and grace. So much the greater and more immediate dependence there is on the divine holiness, so much the greater occasion to take notice of and acknowledge that. So much the greater and more absolute dependence we have on the divine perfections, as belonging to the several persons of the Trinity, so much the greater occasion have we to observe and own the divine glory of each of them. That which we are most concerned with, is surely most in the way of our observation and notice; and this kind of concern with any thing, viz., dependence, does especially tend to commend and oblige the attention and observation. Those things that we are not much dependent upon, 'tis easy to neglect; but we can scarce do any other than mind that which we have a great dependence on. By reason of our so great dependence on God and his perfections, and in so many respects, he and his glory are the more directly set in our view, which way soever we turn our eyes.

We have the greater occasion to take notice of God's all-sufficiency, when all our sufficiency is thus every way of him. We have the more occasion to contemplate him as an infinite good, and as the fountain of all good. Such a dependence on God demonstrates God's all-sufficiency. So much as the dependence of the creature is on God, so much the greater does the creature's emptiness in himself appear to be; and so much the greater the creature's emptiness, so much the greater must the fulness of the Being be who supplies him. Our having all *of* God shows the fulness of his power and grace: our having all *through* him shows the fulness of his merit and worthiness; and our having all *in* him demonstrates his fulness of beauty, love and happiness.

And the redeemed, by reason of the greatness of their dependence on God, han't only so much the greater occasion, but obligation to contemplate and acknowledge the glory and fulness of God. How unreasonable and ungrateful should we be if we did not acknowledge that sufficiency and glory that we do absolutely, immediately and universally depend upon!

2. Hereby is demonstrated how great God's glory is considered comparatively, or as compared with the creature's. By the creature's being thus wholly and universally dependent on God, it appears that the creature is nothing and that God is all. Hereby it appears that God is infinitely above us; that God's strength, and wisdom and holiness are infinitely greater than ours. However great and glorious the creature apprehends God to be, yet if he be not sensible of the difference between God and him, so as to see that God's glory is great, compared with his own, he will not be disposed to give God the glory due to his name. If the creature, in any respect, sets himself upon a level with God, or exalts himself to any competition with him, however he may apprehend that great honor and profound respect may belong to God from those that are more inferior, and at a greater distance, he will not be so sensible of its being due from him. So much the more men exalt themselves, so much the less will they surely be disposed to exalt God. 'Tis certainly a thing that God aims at in the disposition of things in the affair of redemption (if we allow the Scriptures to be a revelation of God's mind), that God should appear full, and man in himself empty, that God should appear all, and man nothing. 'Tis God's declared design that others should not "glory in his presence"; which implies that 'tis his design to advance his own comparative glory. So much the more man "glories in God's presence," so much the less glory is ascribed to God.

3. By its being thus ordered, that the creature should have so absolute and universal a dependence on God, provision is made that God should have our whole souls, and should be the object of our undivided respect. If we had our dependence partly on God and partly on something else, man's respect would be divided to those different things on which he had dependence. Thus it would be if we depended on God only for a part of our good, and on ourselves or some other being for another part: or if we had our good only from God, and through another that was not God, and in something else distinct from both, our hearts would be divided between the good itself, and him from whom, and him through whom we received it. But now there is no occasion for this, God being not only he from or of whom we have all good, but also through whom, and one that is that good itself, that we have from him and through him. So that whatsoever there is to attract our respect, the tendency is still directly towards God, all unites in him as the centre.

USE

1. We may here observe the marvellous wisdom of God in the work of redemption. God hath made man's emptiness and misery, his low, lost and ruined state into which he sunk by the fall, an occasion of the greater advancement of his own glory, as in other ways, so particularly in this, that there is now a much more universal and apparent dependence of man on God. Though God be pleased to lift man out of that dismal abyss of sin and woe into which he was fallen, and exceedingly to exalt him in excellency and honor, and to a high pitch of glory and blessedness, yet the creature hath nothing in any respect to glory of; all the glory evidently belongs to God, all is in a mere and most absolute and divine dependence on the Father, Son and Holy Ghost.

And each person of the Trinity is equally glorified in this work: there is an absolute dependence of the creature on every one for all: all is *of* the Father, all *through* the Son, and all *in* the Holy Ghost. Thus God appears in the work of redemption as *all in all*. It is fit that he that is, and there is none else, should be the Alpha and Omega, the first and the last, the all, and the only, in this work.

2. Hence those doctrines and schemes of divinity that are in any respect opposite to such an absolute and universal dependence on God, do derogate from God's glory, and thwart the design of the contrivance for our redemption. Those schemes that put the creature in God's stead, in any of the mentioned respects, that exalt man into the place of either Father, Son or Holy Ghost, in any thing pertaining to our redemption; that, however they may allow of a dependence of the redeemed on God, yet deny a dependence that is so absolute and universal; that own an entire dependence on God for some things, but not for others; that own that we depend on God for the gift and acceptance of a Redeemer, but deny so absolute a dependence on him for the obtaining of an interest in the Redeemer; that own an absolute dependence on the Father for giving his Son, and on the Son for working out redemption, but not so entire a dependence on the Holy Ghost for conversion and a being in Christ, and so coming to a title to his benefits; that own a dependence on God for means of grace, but not absolutely for the benefit and success of those means; that own a partial dependence on the power of God for the obtaining and exercising holiness, but not a mere dependence on the arbitrary and sovereign grace of God; that own a dependence on the free grace of God for a reception into his favor, so far that it is without any proper merit, but not as it is without being attracted, or moved with any excellency; that own a partial dependence on Christ, as he through whom we have life, as having purchased new terms of life, but still hold that the righteousness through which we have life is inherent in ourselves, as it was under the first covenant; and whatever other way any scheme is inconsistent with our entire dependence on God for all, and in each of those ways, of having all of him, through him, and in him, it is repugnant to the design and tenor of the gospel and robs it of that which God accounts its lustre and glory.

3. Hence we may learn a reason why faith is that by which we come to have an interest in this redemption; for there is included in the nature of faith a sensibleness and acknowledgment of this absolute dependence on God in this affair. 'Tis very fit that it should be required of all, in order to their having the benefit of this redemption, that they should be sensible of, and acknowledge the dependence on God for it. 'Tis by this means that God hath contrived to glorify himself in redemption; and 'tis fit that God should at least have this glory of those that are the subjects of this redemption, and have the benefit of it.

Faith is a sensibleness of what is real in the work of redemption; and as we do really wholly depend on God, so the soul that believes doth entirely depend on God for all salvation, in its own sense and act. Faith abases men and exalts God, it gives all the glory of redemption to God alone. It is necessary in order to saving faith, that man should be emptied of himself, that he should be sensible that he is "wretched, and miserable, and poor, and blind, and naked." Humility is a great ingredient of true faith: he that truly receives redemption, receives it as a little child: Mark x. 15, "Whosoever shall not receive the kingdom of heaven as a little child, he shall not enter therein." It is the delight of a believing soul to abase itself and exalt God alone: that is the language of it, Psalm cxv. 1, "Not unto us, O Lord, not unto us, but to thy name give glory."

4. Let us be exhorted to exalt God alone, and ascribe to him all the glory of redemption. Let us endeavor to obtain, and increase in a sensibleness of our great dependence on God, to have our eye to him alone, to mortify a self-dependent and self-righteous disposition. Man is naturally exceeding prone to be exalting himself and depending on his own power or goodness, as though he were he

from whom he must expect happiness, and to have respect to enjoyments alien from God and his Spirit, as those in which happiness is to be found.

And this doctrine should teach us to exalt God alone, as by trust and reliance, so by praise. *Let him that glorieth, glory in the Lord.* Hath any man hope that he is converted and sanctified, and that his mind is endowed with true excellency and spiritual beauty, and his sins forgiven, and he received into God's favor, and exalted to the honor and blessedness of being his child, and an heir of eternal life: let him give God all the glory; who alone makes him to differ from the worst of men in this world, or the miserablest of the damned in hell. Hath any man much comfort and strong hope of eternal life, let not his hope lift him up, but dispose him the more to abase himself and reflect on his own exceeding unworthiness of such a favor, and to exalt God alone. Is any man eminent in holiness and abundant in good works, let him take nothing of the glory of it to himself, but ascribe it to him whose "workmanship we are, created in Christ Jesus unto good works."

II

A DIVINE AND SUPERNATURAL LIGHT, IMMEDIATELY IMPARTED TO THE SOUL BY THE SPIRIT OF GOD, SHOWN TO BE BOTH A SCRIPTURAL AND RATIONAL DOCTRINE.°

MATT. xvi.—And Jesus answered and said unto him, Blessed art thou, Simon Barjona: for flesh and blood hath not revealed it unto thee, but my Father which is in heaven.

Christ says these words to Peter upon occasion of his professing his faith in him as the Son of God. Our Lord was inquiring of his disciples, who men said he was; not that he needed to be informed, but only to introduce and give occasion to what follows. They answer, that some said he was John the Baptist, and some Elias, and others Jeremias, or one of the Prophets. When they had thus given an account who others said he was, Christ asks them, who they said he was. Simon Peter, whom we find always zealous and forward, was the first to answer: he readily replied to the question, *Thou art Christ, the Son of the living God.*

Upon this occasion, Christ says as he does *to* him, and *of* him in the text: in which we may observe,

1. That Peter is pronounced blessed on this account. *Blessed art Thou.*—"Thou art a happy man, that thou art not ignorant of this, that I am Christ, the Son of the living God. Thou art distinguishingly happy. Others are blinded, and have dark and deluded apprehensions, as you have now given an account, some thinking that I am Elias, and some that I am Jeremias, and some one thing, and some another; but none of them thinking right, all of them misled. Happy art thou, that art so distinguished as to know the truth in this matter."

2. The evidence of this his happiness declared; viz., that God, and he only, had *revealed it* to him. This is an evidence of his being *blessed.*

First, As it shows how peculiarly favored he was of God above others; q. d., "How highly favored art thou, that others that are wise and great men, the Scribes, Pharisees and Rulers, and the nation in general, are left in darkness, to follow their own misguided apprehensions; and that thou shouldst be singled out, as it were, by name, that my Heavenly Father should thus set his love on thee, Simon Barjona. This argues thee blessed, that thou shouldst thus be the object of God's distinguishing love."

Secondly, It evidences his blessedness also, as it intimates that this knowledge is above any that flesh and blood can reveal. "This is such knowledge as my Father which is in heaven only can give: it is too high and excellent to be communicated by such means as other knowledge is. Thou art blessed, that thou knowest that which God alone can teach thee."

The original of this knowledge is here declared, both negatively and positively. Positively, as God is here declared the author of it. Negatively, as it is declared, that flesh and blood had not revealed it. God is the author of all knowledge and understanding whatsoever. He is the author of the knowledge that is obtained by human learning: he is the author of all moral prudence, and of the knowledge and skill that men have in their secular business. Thus it is said of all in Israel that were wise-hearted and skilful in embroidering, that God had filled them with the spirit of wisdom, Exod. xxviii. 3.

God is the author of such knowledge; but yet not so but that flesh and blood reveals it. Mortal men are capable of imparting the knowledge of human arts and sciences, and skill in temporal affairs. God is the author of such knowledge by those means: flesh and blood is made use of by God as the mediate or second cause of it; he conveys it by the power and influence of natural means. But this spiritual knowledge, spoken of in the text, is what God is the author of, and none else: he reveals it, and flesh and blood reveals it not. He imparts this knowledge immediately, not making use of any intermediate natural causes, as he does in other knowledge.

What had passed in the preceding discourse naturally occasioned Christ to observe this; because the disciples had been telling how others did not know him, but were generally mistaken about him, and divided and confounded in their opinions of him: but Peter had declared his assured faith, that he was the Son of God. Now it was natural to observe, how it was not flesh and blood that had revealed it to him, but God: for if this knowledge were dependent on natural causes or means, how came it to pass that they, a company of poor fishermen, illiterate men, and persons of low education, attained to the knowledge of the truth; while the Scribes and Pharisees, men of vastly higher advantages, and greater knowledge and sagacity in other matters, remained in ignorance? This could be owing only to the gracious distinguishing influence and revelation of the Spirit of God. Hence, what I would make the subject of my present discourse from these words is this

DOCTRINE

viz., *That there is such a thing as a Spiritual and Divine Light, immediately imparted to the soul by God, of a different nature from any that is obtained by natural means.*

In what I say on this subject at this time I would

I. Show what this divine light is.

II. How it is given immediately by God, and not obtained by natural means.

III. Show the truth of the doctrine.

And then conclude with a brief improvement.

I. I would show what this spiritual and divine light is. And in order to it, would show,

First, In a few things what it *is not*. And here,

I. *Those convictions that natural men may have of their sin and misery,* is not *this* spiritual and divine light. Men in a natural condition may have convictions of the guilt that lies upon them, and of the anger of God and their danger of divine vengeance. Such convictions are from light or sensibleness of truth. That some sinners have a greater conviction of their guilt and misery than others, is because some have more light, or more of an apprehension of truth than others. And this light and conviction may be from the Spirit of God; the Spirit convinces men of sin: but yet nature is much more concerned in it than in the communication of that spiritual and divine light that is spoken of in the doctrine; 'tis from the Spirit of God only as assisting natural principles, and not as infusing any new principles. Common grace differs from special, in that it influences only by assisting of nature; and not by imparting grace, or bestowing anything above nature. The light that is obtained is wholly natural, or of no superior kind to what mere nature attains to, though more of that kind be obtained than would be obtained if men were left wholly to themselves: or, in other words, common grace only assists the faculties of the soul to do that more fully which they do by nature, as natural conscience or reason will, by mere nature, make a man sensible of guilt, and will accuse and condemn him when he has done amiss. Conscience is a principle natural to men; and the work that it doth naturally, or of itself, is to give an apprehension of right and wrong, and to suggest to the mind the relation that there is between right and wrong and a retribution. The Spirit of God, in those convictions which unregenerate men sometimes have, assists conscience to do this work in a further degree than it would do if they were left to themselves: he helps it against those things that tend to stupefy it, and obstruct its exercise. But in the renewing and sanctifying work of the Holy Ghost, those things are wrought in the soul that are above nature, and of which there is nothing of the like kind in the soul by nature; and they are caused to exist in the soul habitually, and according to such a stated constitution or law that lays such a foundation for exercises in a continued course, as is called a principle of nature. Not only are remaining principles assisted to do their work more freely and fully, but those principles are restored that were utterly destroyed by the fall; and the mind thenceforward habitually exerts those acts that the dominion of sin had made it as wholly destitute of, as a dead body is of vital acts.

The Spirit of God acts in a very different manner in the one case from what he doth in the other. He may indeed act upon the mind of a natural man, but he acts in the mind of a saint as an indwelling vital principle. He acts upon the mind of an unregenerate person as an extrinsic, occasional agent; for in acting upon them, he doth not unite himself to them; notwithstanding all his influences that they may be the subjects of, they are still sensual, having not the Spirit, Jude 19. But he unites himself with the mind of a saint, takes him for his temple, actuates and influences him as a new, supernatural principle of life and action. There is this difference, that the Spirit of God, in acting in the soul of a godly man, exerts and communicates himself there in his own proper nature. Holiness is the proper nature of the Spirit of God. The Holy Spirit operates in the minds of the godly by uniting himself to them, and living in them, and exerting his own nature in the exercise of their faculties. The Spirit of God may act upon a creature, and yet not in acting communicate himself. The Spirit of God may act upon inanimate creatures; as the Spirit moved upon the face of the waters in the beginning of the creation; so the Spirit of God may act upon the minds of men many ways, and communicate himself no more than when he acts upon an inanimate creature. For instance, he may excite thoughts in them, may assist their natural reason and understanding, or may assist other natural principles, and this without any union with the soul, but may act, as it were, as upon an external object. But as he acts in his holy influences and spiritual operations, he acts in a way of peculiar communication of himself; so that the subject is thence denominated spiritual.

2. *This* spiritual and divine light *don't consist in any impression made upon the imagination*. It is no impression upon the mind, as though one saw any thing with the bodily eyes: 'tis no imagination or idea of an outward light or glory, or any beauty of form or countenance, or a visible lustre or brightness of any object. The imagination may be strongly impressed with such things; but this is not spiritual light. Indeed when the mind has a lively discovery of spiritual things, and is greatly affected by the power of divine light, it may, and probably very commonly doth, much affect the imagination; so that impressions of an outward beauty or brightness may accompany those spiritual discoveries. But spiritual light is not that impression upon the imagination, but an exceeding different thing from

it. Natural men may have lively impressions on their imaginations; and we can't determine but that the devil, who transforms himself into an angel of light, may cause imaginations of an outward beauty, or visible glory, and of sounds and speeches and other such things; but these are things of a vastly inferior nature to spiritual light.

3. *This* spiritual light is *not the suggesting of any new truths or propositions not contained in the word of God.* This suggesting of new truths or doctrines to the mind, independent of any antecedent revelation of those propositions, either in word or writing, is inspiration; such as the prophets and apostles had, and such as some enthusiasts pretend to. But this spiritual light that I am speaking of, is quite a different thing from inspiration: it reveals no new doctrine, it suggests no new proposition to the mind, it teaches no new thing of God, or Christ, or another world, not taught in the Bible, but only gives a due apprehension of those things that are taught in the word of God.

4. *'Tis not every affecting view that men have of the things of religion that is this* spiritual and divine light. Men by mere principles of nature are capable of being affected with things that have a special relation to religion as well as other things. A person by mere nature, for instance, may be liable to be affected with the story of Jesus Christ, and the sufferings he underwent, as well as by any other tragical story: he may be the more affected with it from the interest he conceives mankind to have in it: yea, he may be affected with it without believing it; as well as a man may be affected with what he reads in a romance, or sees acted in a stage play. He may be affected with a lively and eloquent description of many pleasant things that attend the state of the blessed in heaven, as well as his imagination be entertained by a romantic description of the pleasantness of fairy-land, or the like. And that common belief of the truth of the things of religion that persons may have from education or otherwise, may help forward their affection. We read in Scripture of many that were greatly affected with things of a religious nature, who yet are there represented as wholly graceless, and many of them very ill men. A person therefore may have affecting views of the things of religion, and yet be very destitute of spiritual light. Flesh and blood may be the author of this: one man may give another an affecting view of divine things with but common assistance; but God alone can give a spiritual discovery of them.

But I proceed to show,

Secondly, Positively what this spiritual and divine light *is.*

And it may be thus described: *a true sense of the divine excellency of the things revealed in the word of God, and a conviction of the truth and reality of them thence arising.*

This spiritual light primarily consists in the former of these, viz., a real sense and apprehension of the divine excellency of things revealed in the word of God. A spiritual and saving conviction of the truth and reality of these things arises from such a sight of their divine excellency and glory; so that this conviction of their truth is an effect and natural consequence of this sight of their divine glory. There is therefore in this spiritual light,

1. *A true sense of the divine and superlative excellency of the things of religion;* a real sense of the excellency of God and Jesus Christ, and of the work of redemption, and the ways and works of God revealed in the gospel. There is a divine and superlative glory in these things; an excellency that is of a

vastly higher kind and more sublime nature than in other things; a glory greatly distinguishing them from all that is earthly and temporal. He that is spiritually enlightened truly apprehends and sees it, or has a sense of it. He does not merely rationally believe that God is glorious, but he has a sense of the gloriousness of God in his heart. There is not only a rational belief that God is holy and that holiness is a good thing, but there is a sense of the loveliness of God's holiness. There is not only a speculatively judging that God is gracious, but a sense how amiable God is upon that account, or a sense of the beauty of this divine attribute.

There is a twofold understanding or knowledge of good that God has made the mind of man capable of. The first, that which is merely speculative or notional; as when a person only speculatively judges that anything is, which, by the agreement of mankind, is called good or excellent, viz., that which is most to general advantage, and between which and a reward there is a suitableness, and the like. And the other is that which consists in the sense of the heart: as when there is a sense of the beauty, amiableness, or sweetness of a thing; so that the heart is sensible of pleasure and delight in the presence of the idea of it. In the former is exercised merely the speculative faculty, or the understanding, strictly so called, or as spoken of in distinction from the will or disposition of the soul. In the latter, the will, or inclination, or heart, are mainly concerned.

Thus there is a difference between having an opinion that God is holy and gracious, and having a sense of the loveliness and beauty of that holiness and grace. There is a difference between having a rational judgment that honey is sweet, and having a sense of its sweetness. A man may have the former, that knows not how honey tastes; but a man can't have the latter unless he has an idea of the taste of honey in his mind. So there is a difference between believing that a person is beautiful, and having a sense of his beauty. The former may be obtained by hearsay, but the latter only by seeing the countenance. There is a wide difference between mere speculative rational judging anything to be excellent, and having a sense of its sweetness and beauty. The former rests only in the head, speculation only is concerned in it; but the heart is concerned in the latter. When the heart is sensible of the beauty and amiableness of a thing, it necessarily feels pleasure in the apprehension. It is implied in a person's being heartily sensible of the loveliness of a thing, that the idea of it is sweet and pleasant to his soul; which is a far different thing from having a rational opinion that it is excellent.

2. There arises from this sense of divine excellency of things contained in the word of God *a conviction of the truth and reality of them*; and that either indirectly or directly.

First, *Indirectly*, and that two ways.

1. As the *prejudices that are in the heart* against the truth of divine things *are hereby removed*; so that the mind becomes susceptive of the due force of rational arguments for their truth. The mind of man is naturally full of prejudices against the truth of divine things: it is full of enmity against the doctrines of the gospel; which is a disadvantage to those arguments that prove their truth, and causes them to lose their force upon the mind. But when a person has discovered to him the divine excellency of Christian doctrines, this destroys the enmity, removes those prejudices, and sanctifies the reason, and causes it to lie open to the force of arguments for their truth.

Hence was the different effect that Christ's miracles had to convince the disciples from what they had to convince the Scribes and Pharisees. Not that they had a stronger reason, or had their reason more improved; but their reason was sanctified, and those blinding prejudices, that the Scribes and Pharisees were under, were removed by the sense they had of the excellency of Christ and his doctrine.

2. It not only removes the hinderances of reason, but *positively helps reason.* It makes even the speculative notions the more lively. It engages the attention of the mind, with the more fixedness and intenseness to that kind of objects; which causes it to have a clearer view of them, and enables it more clearly to see their mutual relations, and occasions it to take more notice of them. The ideas themselves that otherwise are dim and obscure are by this means impressed with the greater strength, and have a light cast upon them; so that the mind can better judge of them: as he that beholds the objects on the face of the earth, when the light of the sun is cast upon them, is under greater advantage to discern them in their true forms and mutual relations than he that sees them in a dim starlight or twilight.

The mind having a sensibleness of the excellency of divine objects, dwells upon them with delight; and the powers of the soul are more awakened and enlivened to employ themselves in the contemplation of them, and exert themselves more fully and much more to the purpose. The beauty and sweetness of the objects draws on the faculties, and draws forth their exercises: so that reason itself is under far greater advantages for its proper and free exercises, and to attain its proper end, free of darkness and delusion. But,

Secondly, A true sense of the divine excellency of the things of God's word doth more *directly* and *immediately* convince of the truth of them; and that because the excellency of these things is so superlative. There is a beauty in them that is so divine and godlike, that is greatly and evidently distinguishing of them from things merely human, or that men are the inventors and authors of; a glory that is so high and great that, when clearly seen, commands assent to their divinity and reality. When there is an actual and lively discovery of this beauty and excellency, it won't allow of any such thought as that it is a human work, or the fruit of men's invention. This evidence that they that are spiritually enlightened have of the truth of the things of religion is a kind of intuitive and immediate evidence. They believe the doctrines of God's word to be divine, because they see divinity in them; i.e., they see a divine, and transcendent, and most evidently distinguishing glory in them; such a glory as, if clearly seen, does not leave room to doubt of their being of God, and not of men.

Such a conviction of the truth of religion as this, arising, these ways, from a sense of the divine excellency of them, is that true spiritual conviction that there is in saving faith. And this original of it is that by which it is most essentially distinguished from that common assent which unregenerate men are capable of.

II. I proceed now to the second thing proposed, viz., to show *how this light is immediately given by God,* and not obtained by natural means. And here,

1. *'Tis not intended that the natural faculties are not made use of in it.* The natural faculties are the subject of this light: and they are the subject in such a manner that they are not merely passive, but active in it; the acts and exercises of man's understanding are concerned and made use of in it. God, in letting in this light into the soul, deals with man according to his nature, or as a rational creature;

and makes use of his human faculties. But yet this light is not the less immediately from God for that; though the faculties are made use of, 'tis as the subject and not as the cause; and that acting of the faculties in it is not the cause, but is either implied in the thing itself (in the light that is imparted) or is the consequence of it: as the use that we make of our eyes in beholding various objects, when the sun arises, is not the cause of the light that discovers those objects to us.

2. *'Tis not intended that outward means have no concern in this affair.* As I have observed already, 'tis not in this affair, as it is in inspiration, where new truths are suggested: for here is by this light only given a due apprehension of the same truths that are revealed in the word of God; and therefore it is not given without the word. The gospel is made use of in this affair: this light is the "light of the glorious gospel of Christ," 2 Cor. iv. 4. The gospel is as a glass, by which this light is conveyed to us, 1 Cor. xiii. 12: "Now we see through a glass."—But,

3. When it is said that this light is given immediately by God, and not obtained by natural means, *hereby is intended, that 'tis given by God without making use of any means that operate by their own power, or a natural force.* God makes use of means; but 'tis not as mediate causes to produce this effect. There are not truly any second causes of it; but it is produced by God immediately. The word of God is no proper cause of this effect: it does not operate by any natural force in it. The word of God is only made use of to convey to the mind the subject matter of this saving instruction: and this indeed it doth convey to us by natural force or influence. It conveys to our minds these and those doctrines; it is the cause of the notion of them in our heads, but not of the sense of the divine excellency of them in our hearts. Indeed a person can't have spiritual light without the word. But that don't argue that the word properly causes that light. The mind can't see the excellency of any doctrine, unless that doctrine be first in the mind; but the seeing of the excellency of the doctrine may be immediately from the Spirit of God; though the conveying of the doctrine or proposition itself may be by the word. So that the notions that are the subject matter of this light are conveyed to the mind by the word of God; but that due sense of the heart, wherein this light formally consists, is immediately by the Spirit of God. As for instance, that notion that there is a Christ, and that Christ is holy and gracious, is conveyed to the mind by the word of God: but the sense of the excellency of Christ by reason of that holiness and grace, is nevertheless immediately the work of the Holy Spirit.—I come now,

III. To show *the truth of the doctrine*; that is, to show that there is such a thing as that spiritual light that has been described, thus immediately let into the mind by God. And here I would show briefly, that this doctrine is both *scriptural* and *rational*.

First, 'Tis *scriptural*. My text is not only full to the purpose, but 'tis a doctrine that the Scripture abounds in. We are there abundantly taught that the saints differ from the ungodly in this, that they have the knowledge of God, and a sight of God, and of Jesus Christ. I shall mention but few texts of many. 1 John iii. 6, "Whosoever sinneth hath not seen him, nor known him." 3 John 11, "He that doeth good is of God: but he that doeth evil hath not seen God." John xiv. 19, "The world seeth me no more; but ye see me." John xvii. 3, "And this is eternal life, that they might know thee the only true God, and Jesus Christ, whom thou hast sent." This knowledge, or sight of God and Christ, can't be a mere speculative knowledge; because it is spoken of as a seeing and knowing wherein they differ from the ungodly. And by these Scriptures it must not only be a different knowledge in degree and circumstances, and different in its effects; but it must be entirely different in nature and kind.

And this light and knowledge is always spoken of as immediately given of God, Matt. xi. 25, 26, 27: "At that time Jesus answered and said, I thank thee, O Father, Lord of heaven and earth, because thou hast hid these things from the wise and prudent, and hast revealed them unto babes. Even so, Father: for so it seemed good in thy sight. All things are delivered unto me of my father: and no man knoweth the Son, but the Father: neither knoweth any man the Father, save the Son, and he to whomsoever the Son will reveal him." Here this effect is ascribed alone to the arbitrary operation and gift of God, bestowing this knowledge on whom he will, and distinguishing those with it, that have the least natural advantage or means for knowledge, even babes, when it is denied to the wise and prudent. And the imparting of the knowledge of God is here appropriated to the Son of God as his sole prerogative. And again, 2 Cor. iv. 6: "For God, who commanded the light to shine out of darkness, hath shined in our hearts, to give the light of the knowledge of the glory of God in the face of Jesus Christ." This plainly shows that there is such a thing as a discovery of the divine superlative glory and excellency of God and Christ, and that peculiar to the saints: and also, that 'tis as immediately from God, as light from the sun: and that 'tis the immediate effect of his power and will; for 'tis compared to God's creating the light by his powerful word in the beginning of the creation; and is said to be by the Spirit of the Lord, in the 18th verse of the preceding chapter. God is spoken of as giving the knowledge of Christ in conversion, as of what before was hidden and unseen in that, Gal. i. 15, 16: "But when it pleased God, who separated me from my mother's womb, and called me by his grace, to reveal his Son in me." The Scripture also speaks plainly of such a knowledge of the word of God as has been described, as the immediate gift of God, Psal. cxix. 18: "Open thou mine eyes, that I may behold wondrous things out of thy law." What could the Psalmist mean when he begged of God to open his eyes? Was he ever blind? Might he not have resort to the law and see every word and sentence in it when he pleased? And what could he mean by those "wondrous things"? Was it the wonderful stories of the creation and deluge, and Israel's passing through the Red Sea, and the like? Were not his eyes open to read these strange things when he would? Doubtless by "wondrous things" in God's law, he had respect to those distinguishing and wonderful excellencies, and marvellous manifestations of the divine perfections and glory, that there was in the commands and doctrines of the word, and those works and counsels of God that were there revealed. So the Scripture speaks of a knowledge of God's dispensation, and covenant of mercy, and way of grace towards his people, as peculiar to the saints, and given only by God, Psal. xxv. 14: "The secret of the Lord is with them that fear him; and he will show them his covenant."

And that a true and saving belief of the truth of religion is that which arises from such a discovery, is also what the Scripture teaches. As John vi. 40: "And this is the will of him that sent me, that every one which seeth the Son, and believeth on him, may have everlasting life;" where it is plain that a true faith is what arises from a spiritual sight of Christ. And John xvii. 6, 7, 8: "I have manifested thy name unto the men which thou gavest me out of the world. Now they have known that all things whatsoever thou hast given me are of thee. For I have given unto them the words which thou gavest me; and they have received them, and have known surely that I came out from thee, and they have believed that thou didst send me;" where Christ's manifesting God's name to the disciples, or giving them the knowledge of God, was that whereby they knew that Christ's doctrine was of God, and that Christ himself was of him, proceeded from him, and was sent by him. Again, John xii. 44, 45, 46:

"Jesus cried and said, He that believeth on me, believeth not on me, but on him that sent me. And he that seeth me seeth him that sent me. I am come a light into the world, that whosoever believeth on me should not abide in darkness." Their believing in Christ, and spiritually seeing him, are spoken of as running parallel.

Christ condemns the Jews, that they did not know that he was the Messiah, and that his doctrine was true, from an inward distinguishing taste and relish of what was divine, in Luke xii. 56, 57. He having there blamed the Jews, that though they could discern the face of the sky and of the earth, and signs of the weather, that yet they could not discern those times—or, as 'tis expressed in Matthew, the signs of those times—he adds, yea, and why even of your own selves judge ye not what is right? i.e., without extrinsic signs. Why have ye not that sense of true excellency, whereby ye may distinguish that which is holy and divine? Why have ye not that savor of the things of God, by which you may see the distinguishing glory and evident divinity of me and my doctrine?

The Apostle Peter mentions it as what gave them (the apostles) good and well grounded assurance of the truth of the gospel, that they had seen the divine glory of Christ, 2 Pet. i. 16: "For we have not followed cunningly devised fables when we made known unto you the power and coming of our Lord Jesus Christ, but were eyewitnesses of his majesty." The apostle has respect to that visible glory of Christ which they saw in his transfiguration: that glory was so divine, having such an ineffable appearance and semblance of divine holiness, majesty and grace, that it evidently denoted him to be a divine person. But if a sight of Christ's outward glory might give a rational assurance of his divinity, why may not an apprehension of his spiritual glory do so too? Doubtless Christ's spiritual glory is in itself as distinguishing, and as plainly showing his divinity, as his outward glory; and a great deal more: for his spiritual glory is that wherein his divinity consists; and the outward glory of his transfiguration showed him to be divine, only as it was a remarkable image or representation of that spiritual glory. Doubtless, therefore, he that has had a clear sight of the spiritual glory of Christ, may say, I have not followed cunningly devised fables, but have been an eyewitness of his majesty, upon as good grounds as the apostle, when he had respect to the outward glory of Christ that he had seen.

But this brings me to what was proposed next, viz., to show that,

Secondly, This doctrine is *rational.*

I. 'Tis rational to suppose that *there is really such an excellency* in divine things, that is so transcendent and exceedingly different from what is in other things, that, if it were seen, would most evidently distinguish them. We cannot rationally doubt but that things that are divine, that appertain to the Supreme Being, are vastly different from things that are human; that there is that godlike, high and glorious excellency in them, that does most remarkably difference them from the things that are of men; insomuch that if the difference were but seen, it would have a convincing, satisfying influence upon any one, that they are what they are, viz., divine. What reason can be offered against it? Unless we would argue, that God is not remarkably distinguished in glory from men.

If Christ should now appear to any one as he did on the mount at his transfiguration; or if he should appear to the world in the glory that he now appears in in heaven as he will do at the day of judgment; without doubt, the glory and majesty that he would appear in, would be such as would satisfy every one that he was a divine person, and that religion was true: and it would be a most reasonable and well grounded conviction too. And why may there not be that stamp of divinity or divine glory on the word of God, on the scheme and doctrine of the gospel, that may be in like manner distinguishing and as rationally convincing, provided it be but seen! 'Tis rational to suppose that when God speaks to the world, there should be something in his word or speech vastly different from men's word. Supposing that God never had spoken to the world, but we had noticed that he was about to do it; that he was about to reveal himself from heaven and speak to us immediately himself, in divine speeches or discourses, as it were from his own mouth, or that he should give us a book of his own inditing: after what manner should we expect that he would speak? Would it not be rational to suppose that his speech would be exceeding different from men's speech, that he should speak like a God; that is, that there should be such an excellency and sublimity in his speech or word, such a stamp of wisdom, holiness, majesty and other divine perfections, that the word of men, yea of the wisest of men, should appear mean and base in comparison of it? Doubtless it would be thought rational to expect this, and unreasonable to think otherwise. When a wise man speaks in the exercise of his wisdom, there is something in every thing he says that is very distinguishable from the talk of a little child. So, without doubt, and much more, is the speech of God (if there be any such thing as the speech of God) to be distinguished from that of the wisest of men; agreeable to Jer. xxiii. 28, 29. God having there been reproving the false prophets that prophesied in his name and pretended that what they spake was his word, when indeed it was their own word, says, "The prophet that hath a dream, let him tell a dream; and he that hath my word, let him speak my word faithfully. What is the chaff to the wheat? saith the Lord. Is not my word like as a fire? saith the Lord; and like a hammer that breaketh the rock in pieces?"

2. If there be such a distinguishing excellency in divine things, 'tis rational to suppose that *there may be such a thing as seeing it.* What should hinder but that it may be seen! It is no argument, that there is no such thing as such a distinguishing excellency, or that, if there be, that it can't be seen, that some don't see it, though they may be discerning men in temporal matters. It is not rational to suppose, if there be any such excellency in divine things, that wicked men should see it. 'Tis not rational to suppose that those whose minds are full of spiritual pollution, and under the power of filthy lusts, should have any relish or sense of divine beauty or excellency; or that their minds should be susceptive of that light that is in its own nature so pure and heavenly. It need not seem at all strange that sin should so blind the mind, seeing that men's particular natural tempers and dispositions will so much blind them in secular matters; as when men's natural temper is melancholy, jealous, fearful, proud, or the like.

3. 'Tis rational to suppose that *this knowledge should be given immediately by God,* and not be obtained by natural means. Upon what account should it seem unreasonable, that there should be any immediate communication between God and the creature? It is strange that men should make any matter of difficulty of it. Why should not he that made all things, still have something immediately to do with the things that he has made? Where lies the great difficulty, if we own the being of a God, and that he created all things out of nothing, of allowing some immediate influence of God on the creation still? And if it be reasonable to suppose it with respect to any part of the creation, it is especially so with respect to reasonable, intelligent creatures; who are next to God in the gradation of the different orders of beings, and whose business is most immediately with God; who were made on purpose for those exercises that do respect God and wherein they have nextly to do with God: for reason teaches, that man was made to serve and glorify his Creator. And if it be

rational to suppose that God immediately communicates himself to man in any affair, it is in this. 'Tis rational to suppose that God would reserve that knowledge and wisdom, that is of such a divine and excellent nature, to be bestowed immediately by himself, and that it should not be left in the power of second causes. Spiritual wisdom and grace is the highest and most excellent gift that ever God bestows on any creature: in this the highest excellency and perfection of a rational creature consists. 'Tis also immensely the most important of all divine gifts: 'tis that wherein man's happiness consists, and on which his everlasting welfare depends. How rational is it to suppose that God, however he has left meaner goods and lower gifts to second causes, and in some sort in their power, yet should reserve this most excellent, divine and important of all divine communications in his own hands, to be bestowed immediately by himself, as a thing too great for second causes to be concerned in! 'Tis rational to suppose that this blessing should be immediately from God; for there is no gift or benefit that is in itself so nearly related to the divine nature, there is nothing the creature receives that is so much of God, of his nature, so much a participation of the deity: 'tis a kind of emanation of God's beauty, and is related to God as the light is to the sun. 'Tis therefore congruous and fit, that when it is given of God, it should be nextly from himself, and by himself, according to his own sovereign will.

'Tis rational to suppose that it should be beyond a man's power to obtain this knowledge and light by the mere strength of natural reason; for 'tis not a thing that belongs to reason, to see the beauty and loveliness of spiritual things; it is not a speculative thing, but depends on the sense of the heart. Reason, indeed, is necessary in order to it, as 'tis by reason only that we are become the subjects of the means of it; which means I have already shown to be necessary in order to it, though they have no proper causal influence in the affair. 'Tis by reason that we become possessed of a notion of those doctrines that are the subject matter of this divine light; and reason may many ways be indirectly and remotely an advantage to it. And reason has also to do in the acts that are immediately consequent on this discovery: a seeing the truth of religion from hence is by reason; though it be but by one step, and the inference be immediate. So reason has to do in that accepting of, and trusting in Christ, that is consequent on it. But if we take reason strictly, not for the faculty of mental perception in general, but for ratiocination, or a power of inferring by arguments; I say, if we take reason thus, the perceiving of spiritual beauty and excellency no more belongs to reason than it belongs to the sense of feeling to perceive colors, or to the power of seeing to perceive the sweetness of food. It is out of reason's province to perceive the beauty or loveliness of any thing: such a perception don't belong to that faculty. Reason's work is to perceive truth and not excellency. It is not ratiocination that gives men the perception of the beauty and amiableness of a countenance, though it may be many ways indirectly an advantage to it; yet 'tis no more reason that immediately perceives it than it is reason that perceives the sweetness of honey: it depends on the sense of the heart. Reason may determine that a countenance is beautiful to others, it may determine that honey is sweet to others; but it will never give me a perception of its sweetness.—I will conclude with a very brief

IMPROVEMENT

of what has been said.

First, This doctrine may lead us to reflect on the goodness of God, that has so ordered it, that a saving evidence of the truth of the gospel is such as is attainable by persons of mean capacities and advantages, as well as those that are of the greatest parts and learning. If the evidence of the gospel depended only on history, and such reasonings as learned men only are capable of, it would be above the reach of far the greatest part of mankind. But persons with but an ordinary degree of knowledge are capable, without a long and subtile train of reasoning, to see the divine excellency of the things of religion: they are capable of being taught by the Spirit of God, as well as learned men. The evidence that is this way obtained is vastly better and more satisfying than all that can be obtained by the arguings of those that are most learned, and greatest masters of reason. And babes are as capable of knowing these things as the wise and prudent; and they are often hid from these when they are revealed to those: 1 Cor. i. 26, 27, "For ye see your calling, brethren, how that not many wise men after the flesh, not many mighty, not many noble, are called. But God hath chosen the foolish things of the world...."

Secondly, This doctrine may well put us upon examining ourselves, whether we have ever had this divine light that has been described let into our souls. If there be such a thing indeed, and it be not only a notion or whimsy of persons of weak and distempered brains, then doubtless 'tis a thing of great importance, whether we have thus been taught by the Spirit of God; whether the light of the glorious gospel of Christ, who is the image of God, hath shined unto us, giving us the light of the knowledge of the glory of God in the face of Jesus Christ; whether we have seen the Son, and believed on him, or have that faith of gospel doctrines that arises from a spiritual sight of Christ.

Thirdly, All may hence be exhorted earnestly to seek this spiritual light. To influence and move to it, the following things may be considered.

1. This is the most *excellent and divine* wisdom that any creature is capable of. 'Tis more excellent than any human learning; 'tis far more excellent than all the knowledge of the greatest philosophers or statesmen. Yea, the least glimpse of the glory of God in the face of Christ doth more exalt and ennoble the soul than all the knowledge of those that have the greatest speculative understanding in divinity without grace. This knowledge has the most noble object that is or can be, viz., the divine glory or excellency of God and Christ. The knowledge of these objects is that wherein consists the most excellent knowledge of the angels, yea, of God himself.

2. This knowledge is that which is above all others *sweet and joyful*. Men have a great deal of pleasure in human knowledge, in studies of natural things; but this is nothing to that joy which arises from this divine light shining into the soul. This light gives a view of those things that are immensely the most exquisitely beautiful, and capable of delighting the eye of the understanding. This spiritual light is the dawning of the light of glory in the heart. There is nothing so powerful as this to support persons in affliction, and to give the mind peace and brightness in this stormy and dark world.

3. This light is such as effectually influences the inclination, and *changes the nature of the soul*. It assimilates the nature to the divine nature, and changes the soul into an image of the same glory that is beheld: 2 Cor. iii. 18, "But we all, with open face, beholding as in a glass the glory of the Lord, are changed into the same image from glory to glory, even as by the Spirit of the Lord." This knowledge will wean from the world and raise the inclination to heavenly things. It will turn the heart to God as the fountain of good, and to choose him for the only portion. This light, and this only, will bring the soul to a saving close with Christ. It conforms the heart to the gospel, mortifies its enmity and opposition against the scheme of salvation therein revealed. It causes the heart to embrace the joyful tidings, and entirely to adhere to, and acquiesce in the revelation of Christ as our Saviour. It causes

the whole soul to accord and symphonize with it, admitting it with entire credit and respect, cleaving to it with full inclination and affection; and it effectually disposes the soul to give up itself entirely to Christ.

4. This light, and this only, *has its fruit in an universal holiness of life.* No merely notional or speculative understanding of the doctrines of religion will ever bring to this. But this light, as it reaches the bottom of the heart, and changes the nature, so it will effectually dispose to an universal obedience. It shows God's worthiness to be obeyed and served. It draws forth the heart in a sincere love to God, which is the only principle of a true, gracious and universal obedience. And it convinces of the reality of those glorious rewards that God has promised to them that obey him.

III

RUTH'S RESOLUTION°

RUTH i. 16.—And Ruth said, Intreat me not to leave thee, or to return from following after thee: for whither thou goest, I will go; and where thou lodgest, I will lodge: thy people shall be my people, and thy God my God.

The historical things in this book of Ruth seem to be inserted into the canon of the Scripture especially on two accounts:

First, Because Christ was of Ruth's posterity. The Holy Ghost thought fit to take particular notice of that marriage of Boaz with Ruth, whence sprang the Saviour of the world. We may often observe it, that the Holy Spirit who indited the Scriptures, often takes notice of little things, minute occurrences, that do but remotely relate to Jesus Christ.

Secondly, Because this history seems to be typical of the calling of the Gentile church, and indeed of the conversion of every believer. Ruth was not originally of Israel, but was a Moabitess, an alien from the commonwealth of Israel: but she forsook her own people, and the idols of the Gentiles, to worship the God of Israel, and to join herself to that people. Herein she seems to be a type of the Gentile church, and also of every sincere convert. Ruth was the mother of Christ; he came of her posterity: so the church is Christ's mother, as she is represented, Rev. xii., at the beginning. And so also is every true Christian his mother: Matt. xii. 50, "Whosoever shall do the will of my Father which is in heaven, the same is my brother, and sister, and mother." Christ is what the soul of every one of the elect is in travail with in the new birth. Ruth forsook all her natural relations and her own country, the land of her nativity, and all her former possessions there, for the sake of the God of Israel; as every true Christian forsakes all for Christ. Psalm xlv. 10, "Hearken, O daughter, and consider, and incline thine ear; forget also thine own people, and thy father's house."

Naomi was now returning out of the land of Moab into the land of Israel with her two daughters in law, Orpah and Ruth; who will represent to us two sorts of professors of religion: Orpah, that sort that indeed make a fair profession, and seem to set out well, but dure but for a while, and then turn back; Ruth, that sort that are sound and sincere, and therefore are steadfast and persevering in the way that they have set out in. Naomi in the preceding verses represents to these her daughters the difficulties of their leaving their own country to go with her. And in this verse may be observed,

1. The remarkable conduct and behavior of Ruth on this occasion; with what inflexible resolution she cleaves to Naomi and follows her. When Naomi first arose to return from the country of Moab into the land of Israel, Orpah and Ruth both set out with her; and Naomi exhorts them both to return. And they both of them wept, and seemed as if they could not bear the thoughts of leaving her, and appeared as if they were resolved to go with her: verse 10, "And they said unto her, Surely we will return with thee unto thy people." Then Naomi says to them again, "Turn again, my daughters, go your way," &c. And then they were greatly affected again, and Orpah returned and went back. Now Ruth's steadfastness in her purpose had a greater trial, but yet is not overcome: "She clave unto her," verse 14. Then Naomi speaks to her again, verse 15, "Behold, thy sister in law is gone back unto her

people, and unto her gods: return thou after thy sister in law." And then she shows her immovable resolution in the text and following verse.

2. I would particularly observe that wherein the virtuousness of this her resolution consists, viz., that it was for the sake of the God of Israel, and that she might be one of his people, that she was thus resolved to cleave to Naomi: "Thy people shall be my people, and thy God my God." It was for God's sake that she did thus; and therefore her so doing is afterwards spoken of as a virtuous behavior in her, chap. ii. 11, 12: "And Boaz answered and said unto her, It hath fully been showed me, all that thou hast done unto thy mother in law since the death of thine husband: and how thou hast left thy father, and thy mother, and the land of thy nativity, and art come unto a people which thou knewest not heretofore. The Lord recompense thy work, and a full reward be given thee of the Lord God of Israel, under whose wings thou art come to trust." She left her father and mother, and the land of her nativity, to come and trust under the shadow of God's wings: and she had indeed a full reward given her, as Boaz wished; for besides immediate spiritual blessings to her own soul and eternal rewards in another world, she was rewarded with plentiful and prosperous outward circumstances in the family of Boaz. And God raised up David and Solomon of her seed, and established the crown of Israel (the people that she chose before her own people) in her posterity; and—which is much more—of her seed he raised up Jesus Christ, in whom all the families of the earth are blessed.

From the words thus opened, I observe this for the subject of my present discourse:

When those that we have formerly been conversant with, are turning to God, and joining themselves to his people, it ought to be our firm resolution, that we will not leave them; but that their people shall be our people, and their God our God.

It sometimes happens, that of those who have been conversant one with another, that have dwelt together as neighbors, and have been often together as companions, or have been united in near relation, and have been together in darkness, bondage and misery in the service of Satan, some are enlightened, and have their minds changed, are made to see the great evil of sin, and have their hearts turned to God, and are influenced by the Holy Spirit of God to leave their company that are on Satan's side to go and join themselves with that blessed company that are with Jesus Christ; they are made willing to forsake the tents of wickedness, to dwell in the land of uprightness with the people of God.

And sometimes this proves a final parting or separation between them and those that they have been formerly conversant with. Though it may be no parting in outward respects, they may still dwell together and may converse one with another; yet in other respects, it sets them at a great distance one from another: one is a child of God, and the other the enemy of God; one is in a miserable, and the other in a happy condition; one is a citizen of the heavenly Zion, the other is under condemnation to hell. They are no longer together in those respects wherein they used to be together. They used to be of one mind to serve sin and do Satan's work; now they are of contrary minds. They used to be together in worldliness and sinful vanity; now they are of exceeding different dispositions. They are separated as they are in different kingdoms; the one remains in the kingdom of darkness, the other is translated into the kingdom of God's dear Son. And sometimes they are finally separated in these respects; while one dwells in the land of Israel, and in the house of God, the other, like Orpah, lives and dies in the land of Moab.

Now 'tis lamentable when it is thus. 'Tis awful being parted so. 'Tis doleful, when of those that have formerly been together in sin, some turn to God, and join themselves with his people, that it should prove a parting between them and their former companions and acquaintance. It should be our firm and inflexible resolution in such a case that it shall be no parting, but that we will follow them, that their people shall be our people, and their God our God; and that for the following reasons:

I. Because their *God* is a glorious God. There is none like him, who is infinite in glory and excellency. He is the most high God, glorious in holiness, fearful in praises, doing wonders. His name is excellent in all the earth, and his glory is above the earth and the heavens. Among the gods there is none like unto him; there is none in heaven to be compared to him, nor are there any among the sons of the mighty that can be likened unto him. Their God is the fountain of all good, and an inexhaustible fountain; he is an all-sufficient God, able to protect and defend them, and do all things for them. He is the King of glory, the Lord strong and mighty, the Lord mighty in battle: a strong rock, and a high tower. There is none like the God of Jeshurun, who rideth on the heaven in their help, and in his excellency on the sky. The eternal God is their refuge, and underneath are everlasting arms. He is a God that hath all things in his hands, and does whatsoever he pleases: he killeth and maketh alive; he bringeth down to the grave and bringeth up; he maketh poor and maketh rich: the pillars of the earth are the Lord's. Their God is an infinitely holy God; there is none holy as the Lord. And he is infinitely good and merciful. Many that others worship and serve as gods are cruel beings, spirits that seek the ruin of souls; but this is a God that delighteth in mercy; his grace is infinite and endures forever. He is love itself, an infinite fountain and ocean of it.

Such a God is their God! Such is the excellency of Jacob! Such is the God of them who have forsaken their sins and are converted! They have made a wise choice who have chosen this for their God. They have made a happy exchange indeed, that have exchanged sin and the world for such a God!

They have an excellent and glorious Saviour, who is the only-begotten Son of God; the brightness of his Father's glory; one in whom God from eternity had infinite delight; a Saviour of infinite love; one that has shed his own blood and made his soul an offering for their sins, and one that is able to save them to the uttermost.

II. Their *people* are an excellent and happy people. God has renewed them, and instamped his own image upon them, and made them partakers of his holiness. They are more excellent than their neighbors, Prov. xii. 26. Yea, they are the excellent of the earth, Psalm xvi. 3. They are lovely in the sight of the angels; and they have their souls adorned with those graces that in the sight of God himself are of great price.

The people of God are the most excellent and happy society in the world. That God whom they have chosen for their God is their Father; he has pardoned all their sins, and they are st peace with him; and he has admitted them to all the privileges of his children. As they have devoted themselves to God, so God has given himself to them. He is become their salvation and their portion: his power and mercy and all his attributes are theirs. They are in a safe state, free from all possibility of perishing: Satan has no power to destroy them. God carries them on eagle's wings, far above Satan's reach, and above the reach of all the enemies of their souls. God is with them in this world; they have his gracious presence. God is for them; who then can be against them? As the mountains are round about Jerusalem, so Jehovah is round about them. God is their shield and their exceeding great reward; and their fellowship is with the Father and with his Son Jesus Christ. And they have the divine promise and oath that in the world to come they shall dwell forever in the glorious presence of God.

It may well be sufficient to induce us to resolve to cleave to those that forsake their sins and idols to join themselves with this people, that God is with them, Zech. viii. 23: "Thus saith the Lord of hosts; In those days it shall come to pass, that ten men shall take hold out of all languages of the nations, even shall take hold of the skirt of him that is a Jew, saying, We will go with you: for we have heard that God is with you." So should persons as it were take hold of the skirt of their neighbors and companions that have turned to God, and resolve that they will go with them, because God is with them.

III. *Happiness* is nowhere else to be had, but in their God, and with their people. There are that are called gods many, and lords many. Some make gods of their pleasures; some choose Mammon for their god; some make gods of their own supposed excellencies, or the outward advantages they have above their neighbors: some choose one thing for their god, and others another. But men can be happy in no other God but the God of Israel: he is the only fountain of happiness. Other gods can't help in calamity; nor can any of them afford what the poor empty soul stands in need of. Let men adore those other gods never so much, and call upon them never so earnestly, and serve them never so diligently, they will nevertheless remain poor, wretched, unsatisfied, undone creatures. All other people are miserable, but that people whose God is the Lord.—The world is divided into two societies. There are the people of God, the little flock of Jesus Christ, that company that we read of, Rev. xiv. 4. "These are they which were not defiled with women; for they are virgins. These are they which follow the Lamb whithersoever he goeth. These were redeemed from among men, being the firstfruits unto God and to the Lamb." And there are those that belong to the kingdom of darkness, that are without Christ, being aliens from the commonwealth of Israel, strangers from the covenant of promise, having no hope, and without God in the world. All that are of this latter company are wretched and undone; they are the enemies of God, and under his wrath and condemnation. They are the devil's slaves, that serve him blindfold, and are befooled and ensnared by him, and hurried along in the broad way to eternal perdition.

IV. When those that we have formerly been conversant with are turning to God, and to his people, their *example* ought to influence us. Their example should be looked upon as the call of God to us to do as they have done. God, when he changes the heart of one, calls upon another; especially does he loudly call on those that have been their friends and acquaintance. We have been influenced by their examples in evil; and shall we cease to follow them when they make the wisest choice that ever they made, and do the best thing that ever they did? If we have been companions with them in worldliness, in vanity, in unprofitable and sinful conversation, it will be a hard case, if there must be a parting now, because we be not willing to be companions with them in holiness and true happiness. Men are greatly influenced by seeing one another's prosperity in other things. If those whom they have been much conversant with grow rich, and obtain any great earthly advantages, it awakens their ambition and eager desire after the like prosperity. How much more should they be influenced, and stirred up to follow them, and be like them, when they obtain that spiritual and eternal happiness that is of infinitely more worth than all the prosperity and glory of this world!

V. Our resolutions to cleave to and follow those that are turning to God, and joining themselves to his people, ought to be *fixed* and *strong*, because of the great difficulty of it. If we will cleave to them, and have their God for our God, and their people for our people, we must mortify and deny all our lusts, and cross every evil appetite and inclination, and forever part with all sin. But our lusts are many and violent. Sin is naturally exceeding dear to us; to part with it is compared to plucking out our right eyes. Men may refrain from wonted ways of sin for a little while, and may deny their lusts in a partial degree, with less difficulty; but 'tis heart-rending work, finally to part with all sin, and to give our dearest lusts a bill of divorce, utterly to send them away. But this we must do, if we would follow those that are truly turning to God. Yea, we must not only forsake sin, but must, in a sense, forsake all the world: Luke xiv. 33, "Whosoever he be of you that forsaketh not all he hath, he cannot be my disciple." That is, he must forsake all in his heart, and must come to a thorough disposition and readiness actually to quit all for God and the glorious spiritual privileges of his people, whenever the case may require it; and that without any prospect of any thing of the like nature, or any worldly thing whatsoever, to make amends for it; and all to go into a strange country, a land that has hitherto been unseen; like Abraham, who being called of God, "went out of his own country, and from his kindred, and from his father's house, for a land that God should show him, not knowing whither he went."

Thus it was a hard thing for Ruth to forsake her native country and her father and mother, her kindred and acquaintance, and all the pleasant things she had in the land of Moab, to dwell in the land of Israel, where she never had been. Naomi told her of the difficulties once and again. They were too hard for her sister Orpah; the consideration of them turned her back after she was set out. Her resolution was not firm enough to overcome them. But so firmly resolved was Ruth, that she broke through all; she was steadfast in it, that, let the difficulty be what it would, she would not leave her mother in law. So persons had need to be very firm in their resolution to conquer the difficulties that are in the way of cleaving to them who are indeed turning from sin to God.

Our cleaving to them, and having their God for our God and their people for our people, depends on our resolution and choice; and that in two respects.

1. The firmness of resolution in using means in order to it, is *the way to have means effectual*. There are means appointed in order to our becoming some of the true Israel and having their God for our God; and the thorough use of these means is the way to have success; but not a slack or slighty use of them. And that we may be thorough, there is need of strength of resolution, a firm and inflexible disposition and bent of mind to be universal in the use of means, and to do what we do with our might, and to persevere in it. Matt. xi. 12, "The kingdom of heaven suffereth violence, and the violent take it by force."

2. A choosing of their God and their people, with a full determination and with the whole soul, is *the condition of an union with them*. God gives every man his choice in this matter: as Orpah and Ruth had their choice, whether they would go with Naomi into the land of Israel, or stay in the land of Moab. A natural man may choose deliverance from hell; but no man doth ever heartily choose God and Christ, and the spiritual benefits that Christ has purchased, and the happiness of God's people, till he is converted. On the contrary, he is averse to them; he has no relish of them; and is wholly ignorant of the inestimable worth and value of them.

Many carnal men do seem to choose these things, but do it not really: as Orpah seemed at first to choose to forsake Moab to go into the land of Israel. But when Naomi came to set before her the difficulty of it, she went back; and thereby showed that she was not fully determined in her choice, and that her whole soul was not in it as Ruth's was.

APPLICATION

The use that I shall make of what has been said is to move sinners to this resolution, with respect to those amongst us that have lately turned to God, and joined themselves to the flock of Christ. Through the abundant mercy and grace of God to us in this place, it may be said of many of you that are in a Christless condition, that you have lately been left by those that were formerly with you in such a state. There are those that you have formerly been conversant with that have lately forsaken a life of sin and the service of Satan, and have turned to God, and fled to Christ, and joined themselves to that blessed company that are with him. They formerly were with you in sin and in misery; but now they are with you no more in that state or manner of life. They are changed, and have fled from the wrath to come; they have chosen a life of holiness here and the enjoyment of God hereafter. They were formerly your associates in bondage, and were with you in Satan's business; but now you have their company no longer in these things. Many of you have seen those you live with, under the same roof, turning from being any longer with you in sin, to be with the people of Jesus Christ. Some of you that are husbands have had your wives; and some of you that are wives have had your husbands; some of you that are children have had your parents; and parents have had your children; many of you have had your brothers and sisters; and many your near neighbors and acquaintance and special friends; many of you that are young have had your companions: I say, many of you have had those that you have been thus concerned with, leaving you, forsaking that doleful life and wretched state that you still continue in. God, of his good pleasure and wonderful grace, hath lately caused it to be so in this place that multitudes have been forsaking their old abodes in the land of Moab, and under the gods of Moab, and going into the land of Israel, to put their trust under the wings of the Lord God of Israel. Though you and they have been nearly related, and have dwelt together, or have been often together and intimately acquainted one with another, they have been taken and you hitherto left. O let it not be the foundation of a final parting! But earnestly follow them; be firm in your resolution in this matter. Don't do as Orpah did, who, though at first she made as though she would follow Naomi, yet when she had the difficulty of it set before her went back: but say as Ruth, "I will not leave thee; but where thou goest, I will go: thy people shall be my people, and thy God my God." Say as she said, and do as she did. Consider the excellency of their God and their Saviour, and the happiness of their people, the blessed state that they are in, and the doleful state that you are in.

You who are old sinners, who have lived long in the service of Satan, have lately seen some that were with you, that have travelled with you in the paths of sin these many years, that with you enjoyed great means and advantages, that have had calls and warnings with you, and have with you passed through remarkable times of the pouring out of God's Spirit in this place, and have hardened their hearts and stood it out with you, and with you have grown old in sin; I say, you have seen some of them turning to God, i.e., you have seen those evidences of it in them, whence you may rationally judge that it is so. O let it not be a final parting! You have been thus long together in sin, and under condemnation; let it be your firm resolution, that, if possible, you will be with them still, now they are in a holy and happy state, and that you will follow them into the holy and pleasant land.

You that tell of your having been seeking salvation for many years, though, without doubt, in a poor dull way, in comparison of what you ought to have done, have seen some that have been with you in that respect, that were old sinners and old seekers, as you are, obtaining mercy. God has lately roused them from their dulness, and caused them to alter their hand, and put them on more thorough endeavors; and they have now, after so long a time, heard God's voice, and have fled for refuge to the Rock of Ages. Let this awaken earnestness and resolution in you. Resolve that you will not leave them.

You that are in your youth, how many have you seen of your age and standing that have of late hopefully chosen God for their God and Christ for their Saviour! You have followed them in sin, and have perhaps followed them into vain company; and will you not now follow them to Christ?

And you that are children, there have lately been some of your sort that have repented of their sins, and have loved the Lord Jesus Christ, and trusted in him, and are become God's children, as we have reason to hope: let it stir you up to resolve to your utmost to seek and cry to God, that you may have the like change made in your hearts, that their people may be your people, and their God your God.

You that are great sinners, that have made yourselves distinguishingly guilty by the wicked practices you have lived in, there are some of your sort that have lately (as we have reason to hope) had their hearts broken for sin, and have forsaken it, and trusted in the blood of Christ for the pardon of it, and have chosen a holy life, and have betaken themselves to the ways of wisdom: let it excite and encourage you resolutely to cleave to them and earnestly to follow them.

Let the following things be here considered:—

1. That your soul is as precious as theirs. It is immortal as theirs is; and stands in as much need of happiness, and can as ill bear eternal misery. You were born in the same miserable condition that they were, having the same wrath of God abiding on you. You must stand before the same Judge; who will be as strict in judgment with you as with them; and your own righteousness will stand you in no more stead before him than theirs; and therefore you stand in as absolute necessity of a Saviour as they. Carnal confidences can no more answer your end than theirs; nor can this world or its enjoyments serve to make you happy without God and Christ more than them. When the bridegroom comes, the foolish virgins stand in as much need of oil as the wise, Matt. xxv. at the beginning.

2. Unless you follow them in their turning to God, their conversion will be a foundation of an eternal separation between you and them. You will be in different interests and in exceeding different states, as long as you live; they the children of God, and you the children of Satan; and you will be parted in another world; when you come to die, there will be a vast separation made between you: Luke xvi. 26, "And besides all this, between us and you there is a great gulf fixed: so that they which would pass from hence to you, cannot; neither can they pass to us, that would come from thence." And you will be parted at the day of judgment. You will be parted at Christ's first appearance in the clouds of heaven. While they are caught up in the clouds to meet the Lord in the air, to be ever with the Lord, you will remain below, confined to this cursed ground, that is kept in store, reserved unto fire, against the day of judgment and perdition of ungodly men. You will appear separated from them while you stand before the great judgment-seat, they being at the right hand, while you are set at the left: Matt. xxv. 32, 33, "And before him shall be gathered all nations: and he shall separate them one from another, as a shepherd divideth his sheep from the goats: and he shall set the sheep on his right hand,

but the goats on the left." And you shall then appear in exceeding different circumstances. While you stand with devils, in the image and deformity of devils, and in ineffable horror and amazement, they shall appear in glory, sitting upon thrones, as assessors with Christ, and as such passing judgment upon you, 1 Cor. vi. 2. And what shame and confusion will then cover you, when so many of your contemporaries, your equals, your neighbors, relations and companions, shall be honored, and openly acknowledged and confessed by the glorious Judge of the universe and Redeemer of saints, and shall be seen by you sitting with him in such glory, and you shall appear to have neglected your salvation, and not to have improved your opportunities, and rejected the Lord Jesus Christ, the same person that will then appear as your great Judge, and you shall be the subjects of wrath, and, as it were, trodden down in eternal contempt and disgrace! Dan. xii. 2, "Some shall rise to everlasting life, and some to shame and everlasting contempt." And what a wide separation will the sentence then passed and executed make between you and them! When you shall be sent away out of the presence of the Judge with indignation and abhorrence, as cursed and loathsome creatures, and they shall be sweetly accosted and invited into his glory as his dear friends and the blessed of his Father! When you, with all that vast throng of wicked and accursed men and devils, shall descend with loud lamentings and horrid shrieks into that dreadful gulf of fire and brimstone, and shall be swallowed up in that great and everlasting furnace, while they shall joyfully, and with sweet songs of glory and praise, ascend with Christ, and all that beauteous and blessed company of saints and angels, into eternal felicity, in the glorious presence of God, and the sweet embraces of his love; and you and they shall spend eternity in such a separation and immensely different circumstances! And that however you have been intimately acquainted and nearly related, closely united and mutually conversant here in this world; and how much soever you have taken delight in each other's company! Shall it be so after you have been together a great while, each of you in undoing yourselves, enhancing your guilt, and heaping up wrath, that their so wisely changing their minds and their course, and choosing such happiness for themselves, should now at length be the beginning of such an exceeding and everlasting separation between you and them? How awful will it be to be parted so!

3. Consider the great encouragement that God gives you, earnestly to strive for the same blessing that others have obtained. There is great encouragement in the word of God to sinners to seek salvation, in the revelation we have of the abundant provision made for the salvation even of the chief of sinners, and in the appointment of so many means to be used with and by sinners, in order to their salvation; and by the blessing which God in his word connects with the means of his appointment. There is hence great encouragement for all, at all times, that will be thorough in using of these means. But now God gives extraordinary encouragement in his providence, by pouring out his Spirit so remarkably amongst us, and bringing savingly home to himself all sorts, young and old, rich and poor, wise and unwise, sober and vicious, old self-righteous seekers and profligate livers: no sort are exempt. There is now at this day amongst us the loudest call and the greatest encouragement and the widest door open to sinners, to escape out of a state of sin and condemnation that perhaps God ever granted in New England. Who is there that has an immortal soul so sottish as not to improve such an opportunity, and that won't bestir himself with all his might now? How unreasonable is negligence, and how exceeding unseasonable is discouragement, at such a day as this! Will you be so stupid as to neglect your soul now? Will any mortal amongst us be so unreasonable as to lag behind, or look back in discouragement when God opens such a door? Let every single person be thoroughly awake! Let every one encourage himself now to press forward, and fly for his life!

4. Consider how earnestly desirous they that have obtained are that you should follow them, and that their people should be your people, and their God your God. They desire that you should partake of that great good that God has given them, and that unspeakable and eternal blessedness that he has promised them. They wish and long for it. If you do not go with them, and are not still of their company, it won't be for want of their willingness, but your own. That of Moses to Hobab is the language of every true saint of your acquaintance to you, Numb. x. 29, "We are journeying unto the place of which the Lord said, I will give it you: come thou with us, and we will do thee good: for the Lord hath spoken good concerning Israel." As Moses, when on his journey through the wilderness, following the pillar of cloud and fire, invited Hobab, that he had been acquainted with and nearly allied to out of the land of Midian, where Moses had formerly dwelt with him, to go with him and his people to Canaan, to partake with them in the good that God had promised them; so do those of your friends and acquaintance invite you, out of a land of darkness and wickedness, where they have formerly been with you, to go with them to the heavenly Canaan. The company of saints, the true church of Christ, invite you. The lovely bride calls you to the marriage supper. She hath authority to invite guests to her own wedding; and you ought to look on her invitation and desire as the call of Christ the bridegroom; for it is the voice of his Spirit in her: Rev. xxii. 17, "The Spirit and the bride say, Come." Where seems to be a reference to what had been said, chap. xix. 7-9, "The marriage of the Lamb is come, and his wife hath made herself ready. And to her was granted that she should be arrayed in fine linen, clean and white: for the fine linen is the righteousness of saints. And he saith unto me, Write, Blessed are they which are called to the marriage supper of the Lamb." 'Tis with respect to this her marriage supper that she, from the motion of the Spirit of the Lamb in her, says, Come. So that you are invited on all hands; all conspire to call you. God the Father invites you: this is the King that has made a marriage for his Son; and he sends forth his servants, the ministers of the gospel, to invite the guests. And the Son himself invites you: 'tis he that speaks, Rev. xvii. 17, "And let him that heareth say, Come; and let him that is athirst, come; and whosoever will, let him come." He tells us who he is in the foregoing verse, "I Jesus, the root and offspring of David, the bright and morning star." And God's ministers invite you, and all the church invites you; and there will be joy in the presence of the angels of God that hour that you accept the invitation.

5. Consider what a doleful company that will be that be left after this extraordinary time of mercy is over. We have reason to think that there will be a number left. We read that when Ezekiel's healing waters increased so abundantly, and the healing effect of them was so very general; yet there were certain places, where the water came, that never were healed: Ezek. xlvii. 9-11, "And it shall come to pass, that every thing that liveth, which moveth, whithersoever the rivers shall come, shall live: and there shall be a very great multitude of fish, because these waters shall come thither: for they shall be healed; and every thing shall live whither the river cometh. And it shall come to pass, that the fishers shall stand upon it from En-gedi even unto En-eglaim; they shall be a place to spread forth nets; their fish shall be according to their kinds, as the fish of the great sea, exceeding many. But the miry places thereof and the marshes thereof shall not be healed; they shall be given to salt." And even in the apostles' times, when there was such wonderful success of the gospel, yet wherever they came, there were some that did not believe: Acts xiii. 48, "And when the Gentiles heard this, they were glad, and glorified the word of the Lord; and as many as were ordained to eternal life, believed." And chap. xxviii. 24, "And some believed, and some believed not." So we have no reason to expect but there will be some left amongst us. 'Tis to be hoped it will be a small company. But what a doleful company will

it be! How darkly and awfully will it look upon them! If you shall be of that company, how well may your friends and relations lament over you, and bemoan your dark and dangerous circumstances! If you would not be one of them, make haste, delay not and look not behind you. Shall all sorts obtain, shall every one press into the kingdom of God, while you stay loitering behind in a doleful undone condition? Shall every one take heaven, while you remain with no other portion but this world? Now take up that resolution, that if it be possible you will cleave to them that have fled for refuge to lay hold of the hope set before them. Count the cost of a thorough, violent, and perpetual pursuit of salvation, and forsake all, as Ruth forsook her own country and all her pleasant enjoyments in it. Don't do as Orpah did; who set out, and then was discouraged, and went back: but hold out with Ruth through all discouragement and opposition. When you consider others that have chosen the better part, let that resolution be ever firm with you: "Where thou goest, I will go; where thou lodgest, I will lodge: thy people shall be my people, and thy God my God."

IV

THE MANY MANSIONS°

JOHN xiv. 2.—In my Father's house are many mansions.

In these words may be observed two things,

1. The thing described, viz., Christ's Father's house. Christ spoke to his disciples in the foregoing chapter as one that was about to leave them. He told 'em, verse 31, "Now is the Son of Man glorified, and God is glorified in him," and then goes to giving of them counsel to live in unity and love one another, as one that was going from them. By which they seemed somewhat surprised and hardly knew what to make of it. And one of them, viz., Peter, asked him where he was going; verse 36, "Simon Peter said unto him, Lord, whither goest thou?" Christ did not directly answer and tell him where he was going, but he signifies where in these words of the text, viz., to his Father's house, i.e., to heaven, and afterwards, in the verse 12, he tells 'em plainly that he was going to his Father.

2. We may observe the description given of it, viz., that in it there are many mansions. The disciples seemed very sorrowful at the news of Christ's going away, but Christ comforts 'em with that, that in his Father's house where he was going there was not only room for him, but room for them too. There were many mansions. There was not only a mansion there for him, but there were mansions enough for them all; there was room enough in heaven for them. When the disciples perceived that Christ was going away, they manifested a great desire to go with him, and particularly Peter. Peter in the latter part of the foregoing chapter asked him whither he went to that end that he might follow him. Christ told him that whither he went he could not follow him now, but that he should follow him afterwards. But Peter, not content with Christ, seemed to have a great mind to follow him now. "Lord," says he, "why cannot I follow thee now?" So that the disciples had a great mind still to be with Christ, and Christ in the words of the text intimates that they shall be with him. Christ signifies to 'em that he was going home to his Father's house, and he encourages 'em that they shall be with him there in due time, in that there were many mansions there. There was a mansion provided not only for him, but for them all (for Judas was not then present), and not only for them, but for all that should ever believe in him to the end of the world; and though he went before, he only went to prepare a place for them that should follow.

The text is a plain sentence; 'tis therefore needless to press any doctrine in other words from it: so that I shall build my discourse on the words of the text. There are two propositions contained in the words, viz., I, that heaven is God's house, and II, that in this house of God there are many mansions.

Prop. I. Heaven is God's house. An house of public worship is an house where God's people meet from time to time to attend on God's ordinances, and that is set apart for that and is called God's house. The temple of Solomon was called God's house. God was represented as dwelling there. There he had his throne in the holy of holies, even the mercy-seat over the ark and between the cherubims.

Sometimes the whole universe is represented in Scripture as God's house, built with various stories one above another: Amos ix. 6, "It is he that buildeth his stories in the heaven;" and Ps. civ. 3, "Who layeth the beams of his chambers in the waters." But the highest heaven is especially represented in Scripture as the house of God. As to other parts of the creation, God hath appointed them to inferior uses; but this part he has reserved for himself for his own abode. We are told that the heavens are the Lord's, but the earth he hath given to the sons of men. God, though he is everywhere present, is represented both in Old Testament and New as being in heaven in a special and peculiar manner. Heaven is the temple of God. Thus we read of God's temple in heaven, Rev. xv. 5. Solomon's temple was a type of heaven; it was made exceeding magnificent and, costly partly to that end, that it might be the most lively type of heaven. The apostle Paul in his epistle to the Hebrews does from time to time call heaven the holy of holies, as being the antitype not only of the temple of Solomon, but of the most holy place in that temple, which was the place of God's most immediate residence: Heb. ix. 12, "He entered in once into the holy place;" verse 24, "For Christ is not entered into the holy places made with hands, which are the figures of the true, but into heaven itself." Houses where assemblies of Christians worship God are in some respects figures of this house of God above. When God is worshipped in them in spirit and truth, they become the outworks of heaven and as it were its gates. As in houses of public worship here there are assemblies of Christians meeting to worship God, so in heaven there is a glorious assembly, or Church, continually worshipping God: Heb. xii. 22, 23, "But ye are come unto mount Sion, the city of the living God, the heavenly Jerusalem, and to an innumerable company of angels, to the general assembly and church of the firstborn, that are written in heaven."

Heaven is represented in Scripture as God's dwelling-house; Ps. cxiii. 5, "Who is like the Lord our God, who dwelleth on high," and Ps. cxxiii. 1, "Unto thee I lift up mine eyes, O thou that dwellest in the heavens." Heaven is God's palace. 'Tis the house of the great King of the universe; there he has his throne, which is therefore represented as his house or temple; Ps. xi. 4, "The Lord is in his holy temple; the Lord's throne is in heaven."

Heaven is the house where God dwells with his family. God is represented in Scripture as having a family; and though some of this family are now on earth, yet in so being they are abroad and not at home, but all going home: Eph. iii. 15, "Of whom the whole family in heaven and earth is named." Heaven is the place that God has built for himself and his children. God has many children, and the place designed for them is heaven; therefore the saints, being the children of God, are said to be of the household of God, Eph. ii. 19: "Now therefore ye are no more strangers and foreigners, but fellow-citizens with the saints, and of the household of God." God is represented as a householder or head of a family, and heaven is his house.

Heaven is the house not only where God hath his throne, but also where he doth as it were keep his table, where his children sit down with him at his table and where they are feasted in a royal manner becoming the children of so great a King: Luke xxii. 30, "That ye may eat and drink at my table in my kingdom;" Matt. xxvi. 29, "But I say unto you, I will not drink henceforth of this fruit of the vine until that day when I drink it new with you in my Father's kingdom."

God is the King of kings, and heaven is the place where he keeps his court. There are his angels and archangels that as the nobles of his court do attend upon him.

Prop. II. There are many mansions in the house of God. By many mansions is meant many seats or places of abode. As it is a king's palace, there are many mansions. Kings' houses are wont to be built very large, with many stately rooms and apartments. So there are many mansions in God's house.

When this is spoken of heaven, it is chiefly to be understood in a figurative sense, and the following things seem to be taught us in it.

I. There is room in this house of God for great numbers. There is room in heaven for a vast multitude, yea, room enough for all mankind that are or ever shall be; Luke xiv. 22, "Lord it is done as thou hast commanded, and yet there is room."

It is not with the heavenly temple as it often is with houses of public worship in this world, that they fill up and become too small and scanty for those that would meet in them, so that there is not convenient room for all. There is room enough in our heavenly Father's house. This is partly what Christ intended in the words of the text, as is evident from the occasion of his speaking them. The disciples manifested a great desire to be where Christ was, and Christ therefore, to encourage them that it should be as they desired, tells them that in his Father's house where he was going were many mansions, i.e., room enough for them.

There is mercy enough in God to admit an innumerable multitude into heaven. There is mercy enough for all, and there is merit enough in Christ to purchase heavenly happiness for millions of millions, for all men that ever were, are or shall be. And there is a sufficiency in the fountain of heaven's happiness to supply and fill and satisfy all: and there is in all respects enough for the happiness of all.

2. There are sufficient and suitable accommodations for all the different sorts of persons that are in the world: for great and small, for high and low, rich and poor, wise and unwise, bond and free, persons of all nations and all conditions and circumstances, for those that have been great sinners as well as for moral livers; for weak saints and those that are babes in Christ as well as for those that are stronger and more grown in grace. There is in heaven a sufficiency for the happiness of every sort; there is a convenient accommodation for every creature that will hearken to the calls of the Gospel. None that will come to Christ, let his condition be what it will, need to fear but that Christ will provide a place suitable for him in heaven.

This seems to be another thing implied in Christ's words. The disciples were persons of very different condition from Christ: he was their Master, and they were his disciples; he was their Lord, and they were the servants; he was their Guide, and they were the followers; he was their Captain, and they the soldiers; he was the Shepherd, and they the sheep; Father, children; he was the glorious, holy Son of God, they were poor, sinful, corrupt men. But yet, though they were in such different circumstances from him, yet Christ encourages them that there shall not only be room in heaven for him, but for them too; for there were many mansions there. There was not only a mansion to accommodate the Lord, but the disciples also; not only the head, but the members; not only the Son of God, but those that are naturally poor, sinful, corrupt men: as in a king's palace there is not only a mansion or room of state built for the king himself and for his eldest son and heir, but there are many rooms, mansions for all his numerous household, children, attendants and servants.

3. It is further implied that heaven is a house that was actually built and prepared for a great multitude. When God made heaven in the beginning of the world, he intended it for an everlasting dwelling-place for a vast and innumerable multitude. When heaven was made, it was intended and prepared for all those particular persons that God had from eternity designed to save: Matt. xxv. 34,

39

"Come, ye blessed prepared for you ." And that is a very great and innumerable multitude: Rev. vii. 9, "After this I beheld, and, lo, a great multitude which no man could number, of all nations, and kindreds, and peoples, and tongues, stood before the throne and before the Lamb, clothed with white robes." Heaven being built designedly for these was built accordingly; it was built so as most conveniently to accommodate all this multitude: as a house that is built for a great family is built large and with many rooms in it; as a palace that is built for a great king that keeps a great court with many attendants is built exceeding great with a great many apartments; and as an house of public worship that is built for a great congregation is built very large with many seats in it.

4. When it is said, , it is meant that there are seats of various dignity and different degrees and circumstances of honor and happiness. There are many mansions in God's house because heaven is intended for various degrees of honor and blessedness. Some are designed to sit in higher places there than others; some are designed to be advanced to higher degrees of honor and glory than others are; and, therefore, there are various mansions, and some more honorable mansions and seats, in heaven than others. Though they are all seats of exceeding honor and blessedness, yet some are more so than others.

Thus a palace is built. Though every part of the palace is magnificent as becomes the palace of a king, yet there are many apartments of various honor, and some are more stately and costly than others, according to the degree of dignity. There is one apartment that is the king's presence-chamber; there are other apartments for the next heir to the crown; there are others for other children; and others for their attendants and the great officers of the household: one for the high steward, and another for the chamberlain, and others for meaner officers and servants.

Another image of this was in Solomon's temple. There were many mansions of different degrees of honor and dignity. There was the holy of holies, where the ark was that was the place of God's immediate residence, where the high priest alone might come; and there was another apartment called the holy place, where the other priests might come; and next to that was the inner court of the temple, where the Levites were admitted: and there they had many chambers or mansions built for lodging-rooms for the priests; and next to that was the court of Israel where the people of Israel might come; and next to that was the court of the Gentiles where the Gentiles, those that were called the "Proselytes of the Gate," might come.

And we have an image of this in houses built for the worship of Christian assemblies. In such houses of God there are many seats of different honor and dignity, from the most honorable to the most inferior of the congregation.

Not that we are to understand the words of Christ so much in a literal sense, as that every saint in heaven was to have a certain seat or room or place of abode where he was to be locally fixed. 'Tis not the design of the Scriptures to inform us much about the external circumstances of heaven or the state of heaven locally considered; but we are to understand what Christ says chiefly in a spiritual sense. Persons shall be set in different degrees of honor and glory in heaven, as is abundantly manifested in Scripture: which may fitly be represented to our imaginations by there being different seats of various honor, as it was in the temple, as it is in kings' courts. Some seats shall be nearer the throne than others. Some shall sit next to Christ in glory: Matt. xx. 23, "To sit on my right hand and on my left, is not mine to give, but it shall be given to them for whom it is prepared of my Father."

Christ has doubtless respect to these different degrees of glory in the text. When he was going to heaven and the disciples were sorrowful at the thoughts of parting with their Lord, he lets them know that there are seats or mansions of various degrees of honor in his Father's house, that there was not only one for him, who was the Head of the Church and the elder brother, but also for them that were his disciples and younger brethren.

Christ also may probably have respect not only to different degrees of glory in heaven, but different circumstances. Though the employment and happiness of all the heavenly assembly shall in the general be the same, yet 'tis not improbable that there may be circumstantial difference. We know what their employment in general, but not in particular. We know not how one may be employed to subserve and promote the happiness of another, and all to help one another. Some may there be set in one place for one office or employment, and others another, as 'tis in the Church on earth. God hath set every one in the body as it hath pleased him; one is the eye, another the ear, another the head, etc. But because God has not been pleased expressly to reveal how it shall be in this respect, therefore I shall not insist upon it, but pass to make some

IMPROVEMENT

of what has been offered.

I. Here is encouragement for sinners that are concerned and exercised for the salvation of their souls, such as are afraid that they shall never go to heaven or be admitted to any place of abode there, and are sensible that they are hitherto in a doleful state and condition in that they are out of Christ, and so have no right to any inheritance in heaven, but are in danger of going to hell and having their place of eternal abode fixed there. You may be encouraged by what has been said, earnestly to seek heaven; for there are many mansions there. There is room enough there. Let your case be what it will, there is suitable provision there for you; and if you come to Christ, you need not fear but that he will prepare a place for you; he'll see to it that you shall be well accommodated in heaven.

But II. I would improve this doctrine in a twofold exhortation.

1. Let all be hence exhorted earnestly to seek that they may be admitted to a mansion in heaven. You have heard that this is God's house; it is his temple. If David, when he was in the wilderness of Judah and in the land of Geshur and of the Philistines, so longed that he might again return into the land of Israel that he might have a place in the house of God here on earth, and prized a place there so much, though it was but that of a door-keeper, how great a happiness will it be to have a place in this heavenly temple of God! If they are looked upon as enjoying a high privilege that have a seat appointed them in kings' courts or in apartments in kings' palaces, especially those that have an abode there in the quality of the king's children, then how great a privilege will it be to have an apartment or mansion assigned to us in God's heavenly palace, and to have a place there as his children! How great is their glory and honor that are admitted to be of the household of God!

And seeing there are many mansions there, mansions enough for us all, our folly will be the greater if we neglect to seek a place in heaven, having our minds foolishly taken up about the worthless, fading things of this world. Here consider three things:

(1) How little a while you can have any mansion or place of abode in this world. Now you have a dwelling amongst the living. You have a house or mansion of your own, or at least one that is at present for your use, and now you have a seat in the house of God; but how little a while will this continue! In a very little while, and the place that now knows you in this world will know you no more. The habitation you have here will be empty of you; you will be carried dead out of it, or shall die at a distance from it, and never enter into it any more, or into any other abode in this world. Your mansion or place of abode in this world, however convenient or commodious it may be, is but as a tent that shall soon be taken down, but a lodge in a garden of cucumbers. Your stay is as it were but for a night. Your body itself is but a house of clay which will quickly moulder and tumble down, and you shall have no other habitation here in this world but the grave.

Thus God in his providence is putting you in mind by the repeated instances of death that have been in the town within the two weeks past, both in one house: in which death he has shown his dominion over old and young. The son was taken away first before the father, being in his full strength and flower of his days; and the father, who was then well and having no appearance of approaching death, followed in a few days: and their habitation and their seat in the house of God in this world will know them no more.

Take warning by these warnings of Providence to improve your time that you may have a mansion in heaven. We have a house of worship newly created amongst us which now you have a seat in, and probably are pleased with the ornaments of it; and though you have a place in so comely a house, yet you know not how little a while you shall have a place in this house of God. Here are a couple snatched away by death that had met in it but a few times, that have been snatched out of it before it was fully finished and never will have any more a seat in it. You know not how soon you may follow, and then of great importance will it be to you to have a seat in God's house above. Both of the persons lately deceased were much on their death-beds warning others to improve their precious time. The first of them was much in expressing his sense of the vast importance of an interest in Christ, as I was a witness, and was earnest in calling on others to improve their time, to be thorough, to get an interest in Christ, and seemed very desirous that young people might receive council and warning from him, as the words of a dying man, to do their utmost to make sure of conversion; and a little before he died left a request to me that I would warn the young people in his room. God has been warning of you in his death and the death of his father that so soon followed. The words of dying persons should be of special weight with us, for then they are in circumstances wherein they are most capable to look on things as they are and judge aright of 'em,—between both worlds as it were. Still that we must all be in.

Let our young people, therefore, take warning from hence, and don't be such fools as to neglect seeking a place and mansion in heaven. Young persons are especially apt to be taken with the pleasing things of this world. You are now, it may be, much pleased with hopes of your future circumstances in this world; pleased with the ornaments of that house of worship that you with others have a place in. But, alas, do you not too little consider how soon you may be taken away from all these things, and no more forever have any part in any mansion or house or enjoyment or happiness under the sun? Therefore let it be your main care to secure an everlasting habitation for hereafter.

(2) Consider when you die, if you have no mansion in the house of God in heaven, you must have your place of abode in the habitation of devils. There is no middle place between them, and when you go hence, you must go to one or the other of these. Some have a mansion prepared for them in heaven from the foundation ; others are sent away as cursed into everlasting burnings prepared for the . Consider how miserable those must be that shall have their habitation with devils to all eternity. Devils are foul spirits; God's great enemies. Their habitation is the blackness of darkness; a place of the utmost filthiness, abomination, darkness, disgrace and torment. O, how would you rather ten thousand times have no place of abode at all, have no being, than to have a place !

(3) If you die unconverted, you will have the worse place in hell for having had a seat or place in God's house in this world. As there are many mansions, places of different degrees of honor in heaven, so there are various abodes and places or degrees of torment and misery in hell; and those will have the worst place there that . Solomon speaks of a peculiarly awful sight that he had seen, that of a wicked man buried that had gone , Eccl. viii. 10. Such as have had a seat in God's house, have been in a sense exalted up to heaven, set on the gate of heaven, cast down to hell.

2. The second exhortation that I would offer from what has been said is to seek a high place in heaven. Seeing there are many mansions of different degrees of honor and dignity in heaven, let us seek to obtain a mansion of distinguished glory. 'Tis revealed to us that there are different degrees of glory to that end that we might seek after the higher degrees. God offered high degrees of glory to that end, that we might seek them by eminent holiness and good works: 2 Cor. ix. 6, "He that sows sparingly ." It is not becoming persons to be over anxious about an high seat in God's house in this world, for that is the honor that is of men; but we can't too earnestly seek after an high seat in God's house above, by seeking eminent holiness, for that is the honor that is of God.

'Tis very little worth the while for us to pursue after honor in this world, where the greatest honor is but a bubble and will soon vanish away, and death will level all. Some have more stately houses than others, and some are in higher office than others, and some are richer than others and have higher seats in the meeting-house than others; but all graves are upon a level. One rotting, putrefying corpse is as ignoble as another; the worms are as bold with one carcass as another.

But the mansions in God's house above are everlasting mansions. Those that have seats allotted 'em there, whether of greater or lesser dignity, whether nearer or further from the throne, will hold 'em to all eternity. This is promised, Rev. iii. 12: "Him that overcometh I will make him a pillar in the temple ." If it be worth the while to desire and seek high seats in the meeting-house, where you are one day in a week, and where you shall never come but few days in all; if it be worth the while much to prize one seat above another in the house of worship only because it is the pew or seat that is ranked first in number, and to be seen here for a few days, how will it be worth the while to seek an high mansion in God's temple and in that glorious place that is the everlasting habitation of God and all his children! You that are pleased with your seats in this house because you are seated high or in a place that is looked upon honorable by those that sit round about, and because many can behold you, consider how short a time you will enjoy this pleasure. And if there be any that are not suited in their seats because they are too low for them, let them consider that it is but a very little while before it will all one to you whether you have sat high or low here. But it will be of infinite and everlasting concern to you where your seat is in another world. Let your great concern be while in this world so to improve your opportunities in God's house in this world, whether you sit high or low, as that you may have a distinguished and glorious mansion in God's house in heaven, where you may be fixed in your place in that glorious assembly in an everlasting rest.

Let the main thing that we prize in God's house be, not the outward ornaments of it, or a high seat in it, but the word of God and his ordinances in it. And spend your time here in seeking Christ, that he may prepare a place for you in his Father's house, that when he comes again to this world, he may take you to himself, that where he is, there you may be also.

V

SINNERS IN THE HANDS OF AN ANGRY GOD°

DEUTERONOMY xxxii. 35.—Their foot shall slide in due time.

In this verse is threatened the vengeance of God on the wicked unbelieving Israelites, that were God's visible people, and lived under means of grace; and that notwithstanding all God's wonderful works that he had wrought towards that people, yet remained, as is expressed verse 28, void of counsel, having no understanding in them; and that, under all the cultivations of heaven, brought forth bitter and poisonous fruit; as in the two verses next preceding the text.

The expression that I have chosen for my text, *their foot shall slide in due time*, seems to imply the following things relating to the punishment and destruction that these wicked Israelites were exposed to.

1. That they were *always* exposed to destruction; as one that stands or walks in slippery places is always exposed to fall. This is implied in the manner of their destruction's coming upon them, being represented by their foot's sliding. The same is expressed, Psalm lxxiii. 18: "Surely thou didst set them in slippery places; thou castedst them down into destruction."

2. It implies that they were always exposed to *sudden*, unexpected destruction; as he that walks in slippery places is every moment liable to fall, he can't foresee one moment whether he shall stand or fall the next; and when he does fall, he falls at once, without warning, which is also expressed in that Psalm lxxiii. 18, 19: "Surely thou didst set them in slippery places: thou castedst them down into destruction. How are they brought into desolation, as *in a moment*!"

3. Another thing implied is, that they are liable to fall of *themselves*, without being thrown down by the hand of another; as he that stands or walks on slippery ground needs nothing but his own weight to throw him down.

4. That the reason why they are not fallen already, and don't fall now, is only that God's appointed time is not come. For it is said that when that due time, or appointed time comes, *their foot shall slide*. Then they shall be left to fall, as they are inclined by their own weight. God won't hold them up in these slippery places any longer, but will let them go; and then, at that very instant, they shall fall to destruction; as he that stands in such slippery declining ground on the edge of a pit that he can't stand alone, when he is let go he immediately falls and is lost.

The observation from the words that I would now insist upon is this,

There is nothing that keeps wicked men at any one moment out of hell, but the mere pleasure of God.

By the mere pleasure of God, I mean his sovereign pleasure, his arbitrary will, restrained by no obligation, hindered by no manner of difficulty, any more than if nothing else but God's mere will had in the least degree or in any respect whatsoever any hand in the preservation of wicked men one moment.

The truth of this observation may appear by the following considerations.

1. There is no want of *power* in God to cast wicked men into hell at any moment. Men's hands can't be strong when God rises up: the strongest have no power to resist him, nor can any deliver out of his hands.

He is not only able to cast wicked men into hell, but he can most easily do it. Sometimes an earthly prince meets with a great deal of difficulty to subdue a rebel that has found means to fortify himself, and has made himself strong by the number of his followers. But it is not so with God. There is no fortress that is any defence against the power of God. Though hand join in hand, and vast multitudes of God's enemies combine and associate themselves, they are easily broken in pieces: they are as great heaps of light chaff before the whirlwind; or large quantities of dry stubble before devouring flames. We find it easy to tread on and crush a worm that we see crawling on the earth; so 'tis easy for us to cut or singe a slender thread that any thing hangs by; thus easy is it for God, when he pleases, to cast his enemies down to hell. What are we, that we should think to stand before him, at whose rebuke the earth trembles, and before whom the rocks are thrown down!

2. They *deserve* to be cast into hell; so that divine justice never stands in the way, it makes no objection against God's using his power at any moment to destroy them. Yea, on the contrary, justice calls aloud for an infinite punishment of their sins. Divine justice says of the tree that brings forth such grapes of Sodom, "Cut it down, why cumbereth it the ground?" Luke xiii. 7. The sword of divine justice is every moment brandished over their heads, and 'tis nothing but the hand of arbitrary mercy, and God's mere will, that holds it back.

3. They are *already* under a sentence of condemnation to hell. They don't only justly deserve to be cast down thither, but the sentence of the law of God, that eternal and immutable rule of righteousness that God has fixed between him and mankind, is gone out against them, and stands against them; so that they are bound over already to hell: John iii. 18, "He that believeth not is condemned already." So that every unconverted man properly belongs to hell; that is his place; from thence he is: John viii. 23, "Ye are from beneath:" and thither he is bound; 'tis the place that justice, and God's word, and the sentence of his unchangeable law, assigns to him.

They are now the objects of that very *same* anger and wrath of God, that is expressed in the torments of hell: and the reason why they don't go down to hell at each moment is not because God, in whose power they are, is not then very angry with them; as angry as he is with many of those miserable creatures that he is now tormenting in hell, and do there feel and bear the fierceness of his wrath. Yea, God is a great deal more angry with great numbers that are now on earth, yea, doubtless, with many that are now in this congregation, that, it may be, are at ease and quiet, than he is with many of those that are now in the flames of hell.

So that it is not because God is unmindful of their wickedness, and don't resent it, that he don't let loose his hand and cut them off. God is not altogether such a one as themselves, though they may imagine him to be so. The wrath of God burns against them; their damnation don't slumber; the pit is prepared; the fire is made ready; the furnace is now hot, ready to receive them; the flames do now rage and glow. The glittering sword is whet, and held over them, and the pit hath opened her mouth under them.

5. The *devil* stands ready to fall upon them, and seize them as his own, at what moment God shall permit him. They belong to him; he has their souls in his possession, and under his dominion. The Scripture represents them as his *goods*, Luke xi. 21. The devils watch them; they are ever by them, at their right hand; they stand waiting for them, like greedy hungry lions that see their prey, and expect to have it, but are for the present kept back; if God should withdraw his hand by which they are restrained, they would in one moment fly upon their poor souls. The old serpent is gaping for them; hell opens its mouth wide to receive them; and if God should permit it, they would be hastily swallowed up and lost.

6. There are in the souls of wicked men those hellish *principles* reigning, that would presently kindle and flame out into hell-fire, if it were not for God's restraints. There is laid in the very nature of carnal men a foundation for the torments of hell: there are those corrupt principles, in reigning power in them, and in full possession of them, that are seeds of hell-fire. These principles are active and powerful, exceeding violent in their nature, and if it were not for the restraining hand of God upon them, they would soon break out, they would flame out after the same manner as the same corruptions, the same enmity does in the heart of damned souls, and would beget the same torments in 'em as they do in them. The souls of the wicked are in Scripture compared to the troubled sea, Isaiah lvii. 20. For the present God restrains their wickedness by his mighty power, as he does the raging waves of the troubled sea, saying, "Hitherto shalt thou come, and no further;" but if God should withdraw that restraining power, it would soon carry all afore it. Sin is the ruin and misery of the soul; it is destructive in its nature; and if God should leave it without restraint, there would need nothing else to make the soul perfectly miserable. The corruption of the heart of man is a thing that is immoderate and boundless in its fury; and while wicked men live here, it is like fire pent up by God's restraints, whenas if it were let loose, it would set on fire the course of nature; and as the heart is now a sink of sin, so, if sin was not restrained, it would immediately turn the soul into a fiery oven, or a furnace of fire and brimstone.

7. It is no security to wicked men for one moment, that there are no *visible means of death* at hand. 'Tis no security to a natural man, that he is now in health, and that he don't see which way he should now immediately go out of the world by any accident, and that there is no visible danger in any respect in his circumstances. The manifold and continual experience of the world in all ages shows that this is no evidence that a man is not on the very brink of eternity, and that the next step won't be into another world. The unseen, unthought of ways and means of persons' going suddenly out of the world are innumerable and inconceivable. Unconverted men walk over the pit of hell on a rotten covering, and there are innumerable places in this covering so weak that they won't bear their weight, and these places are not seen. The arrows of death fly unseen at noonday; the sharpest sight can't discern them. God has so many different, unsearchable ways of taking wicked men out of the world and sending 'em to hell, that there is nothing to make it appear that God had need to be at the expense of a miracle, or go out of the ordinary course of his providence, to destroy any wicked man, at any moment. All the means that there are of sinners' going out of the world are so in God's hands, and so absolutely subject to his power and determination, that it don't depend at all less on the mere will of God, whether sinners shall at any moment go to hell, than if means were never made use of, or at all concerned in the case.

8. Natural men's *prudence* and *care* to preserve their own *lives*, or the care of others to preserve them, don't secure 'em a moment. This, divine providence and universal experience does also bear testimony to. There is this clear evidence that men's own wisdom is no security to them from death; that if it were otherwise we should see some difference between the wise and politic men of the world and others, with regard to their liableness to early and unexpected death; but how is it in fact? Eccles. ii. 16, "How dieth the wise man? As the fool."

9. All wicked men's *pains* and *contrivance* they use to escape *hell*, while they continue to reject Christ, and so remain wicked men, don't secure 'em from hell one moment. Almost every natural man that hears of hell flatters himself that he shall escape it; he depends upon himself for his own security, he flatters himself in what he has done, in what he is now doing, or what he intends to do; every one lays out matters in his own mind how he shall avoid damnation, and flatters himself that he contrives well for himself, and that his schemes won't fail. They hear indeed that there are but few saved, and that the bigger part of men that have died heretofore are gone to hell; but each one imagines that he lays out matters better for his own escape than others have done: he don't intend to come to that place of torment; he says within himself, that he intends to take care that shall be effectual, and to order matters so for himself as not to fail.

But the foolish children of men do miserably delude themselves in their own schemes, and in their confidence in their own strength and wisdom; they trust to nothing but a shadow. The bigger part of those that heretofore have lived under the same means of grace, and are now dead, are undoubtedly gone to hell; and it was not because they were not as wise as those that are now alive; it was not because they did not lay out matters as well for themselves to secure their own escape. If it were so that we could come to speak with them, and could inquire of them, one by one, whether they expected, when alive, and when they used to hear about hell, ever to be subjects of that misery, we, doubtless, should hear one and another reply, "No, I never intended to come here: I had laid out matters otherwise in my mind; I thought I should contrive well for myself: I thought my scheme good: I intended to take effectual care; but it came upon me unexpected; I did not look for it at that time, and in that manner; it came as a thief: death outwitted me: God's wrath was too quick for me. O my cursed foolishness! I was flattering myself, and pleasing myself with vain dreams of what I would do hereafter; and when I was saying peace and safety, then sudden destruction came upon me."

10. God has laid himself under *no obligation*, by any promise, to keep any natural man out of hell one moment. God certainly has made no promises either of eternal life, or of any deliverance or preservation from eternal death, but what are contained in the covenant of grace, the promises that are given in Christ, in whom all the promises are yea and amen. But surely they have no interest in the promises of the covenant of grace that are not the children of the covenant, and that do not believe in any of the promises of the covenant, and have no interest in the Mediator of the covenant.

So that, whatever some have imagined and pretended about promises made to natural men's earnest seeking and knocking, 'tis plain and manifest, that whatever pains a natural man takes in religion, whatever prayers he makes, till he believes in Christ, God is under no manner of obligation to keep him a moment from eternal destruction.

So that thus it is, that natural men are held in the hand of God over the pit of hell; they have deserved the fiery pit, and are already sentenced to it; and God is dreadfully provoked, his anger is as great towards them as to those that are actually suffering the executions of the fierceness of his wrath in hell, and they have done nothing in the least to appease or abate that anger, neither is God in the least bound by any promise to hold 'em up one moment; the devil is waiting for them, hell is gaping for them, the flames gather and flash about them, and would fain lay hold on them and swallow them up; the fire pent up in their own hearts is struggling to break out; and they have no interest in any Mediator, there are no means within reach that can be any security to them. In short they have no refuge, nothing to take hold of; all that preserves them every moment is the mere arbitrary will, and uncovenanted, unobliged forbearance of an incensed God.

APPLICATION

The use may be of *awakening* to unconverted persons in this congregation. This that you have heard is the case of every one of you that are out of Christ. That world of misery, that lake of burning brimstone, is extended abroad under you. *There* is the dreadful pit of the glowing flames of the wrath of God; there is hell's wide gaping mouth open; and you have nothing to stand upon, nor any thing to take hold of. There is nothing between you and hell but the air; 'tis only the power and mere pleasure of God that holds you up.

You probably are not sensible of this; you find you are kept out of hell, but don't see the hand of God in it, but look at other things, as the good state of your bodily constitution, your care of your own life, and the means you use for your own preservation. But indeed these things are nothing; if God should withdraw his hand, they would avail no more to keep you from falling than the thin air to hold up a person that is suspended in it.

Your wickedness makes you as it were heavy as lead, and to tend downwards with great weight and pressure towards hell; and if God should let you go, you would immediately sink and swiftly descend and plunge into the bottomless gulf, and your healthy constitution, and your own care and prudence, and best contrivance, and all your righteousness, would have no more influence to uphold you and keep you out of hell than a spider's web would have to stop a falling rock. Were it not that so is the sovereign pleasure of God, the earth would not bear you one moment; for you are a burden to it; the creation groans with you; the creature is made subject to the bondage of your corruption, not willingly; the sun don't willingly shine upon you to give you light to serve sin and Satan; the earth don't willingly yield her increase to satisfy your lusts; nor is it willingly a stage for your wickedness to be acted upon; the air don't willingly serve you for breath to maintain the flame of life in your vitals, while you spend your life in the service of God's enemies. God's creatures are good, and were made for men to serve God with, and don't willingly subserve to any other purpose, and groan when they are abused to purposes so directly contrary to their nature and end. And the world would spew you out, were it not for the sovereign hand of him who hath subjected it in hope. There are the black clouds of God's wrath now hanging directly over your heads, full of the dreadful storm, and big with thunder; and were it not for the restraining hand of God, it would immediately burst forth upon you. The sovereign pleasure of God, for the present, stays his rough wind; otherwise it would come with fury, and your destruction would come like a whirlwind, and you would be like the chaff of the summer threshing floor.

The wrath of God is like great waters that are dammed for the present; they increase more and more, and rise higher and higher, till an outlet is given; and the longer the stream is stopped, the more rapid and mighty is its course, when once it is let loose. 'Tis true, that judgment against your evil work has not been executed hitherto; the floods of God's vengeance have been withheld; but your guilt in the mean time is constantly increasing, and you are every day treasuring up more wrath; the waters are continually rising, and waxing more and more mighty; and there is nothing but the mere pleasure of God that holds the waters back, that are unwilling to be stopped, and press hard to go forward. If God should only withdraw his hand from the floodgate, it would immediately fly open, and the fiery floods of the fierceness and wrath of God would rush forth with inconceivable fury, and would come upon you with omnipotent power; and if your strength were ten thousand times greater than it is, yea, ten thousand times greater than the strength of the stoutest, sturdiest devil in hell, it would be nothing to withstand or endure it.

The bow of God's wrath is bent, and the arrow made ready on the string, and justice bends the arrow at your heart, and strains the bow, and it is nothing but the mere pleasure of God, and that of an angry God, without any promise or obligation at all, that keeps the arrow one moment from being made drunk with your blood.

Thus are all you that never passed under a great change of heart by the mighty power of the Spirit of God upon your souls; all that were never born again, and made new creatures, and raised from being dead in sin to a state of new and before altogether unexperienced light and life, (however you may have reformed your life in many things, and may have had religious affections, and may keep up a form of religion in your families and closets, and in the house of God, and may be strict in it), you are thus in the hands of an angry God; 'tis nothing but his mere pleasure that keeps you from being this moment swallowed up in everlasting destruction.

However unconvinced you may now be of the truth of what you hear, by and by you will be fully convinced of it. Those that are gone from being in the like circumstances with you see that it was so with them; for destruction came suddenly upon most of them; when they expected nothing of it, and while they were saying, Peace and safety: now they see, that those things that they depended on for peace and safety were nothing but thin air and empty shadows.

The God that holds you over the pit of hell, much as one holds a spider or some loathsome insect over the fire, abhors you, and is dreadfully provoked; his wrath towards you burns like fire; he looks upon you as worthy of nothing else, but to be cast into the fire; he is of purer eyes than to bear to have you in his sight; you are ten thousand times so abominable in his eyes, as the most hateful and venomous serpent is in ours. You have offended him infinitely more than ever a stubborn rebel did his prince: and yet it is nothing but his hand that holds you from falling into the fire every moment. 'Tis ascribed to nothing else, that you did not go to hell the last night; that you was suffered to awake again in this world after you closed your eyes to sleep; and there is no other reason to be given why you have not dropped into hell since you arose in the morning, but that God's hand has held you up. There is no other reason to be given why you han't gone to hell since you have sat here in the house of God, provoking his pure eyes by your sinful wicked manner of attending his solemn worship. Yea, there is nothing else that is to be given as a reason why you don't this very moment drop down into hell.°

O sinner! consider the fearful danger you are in. 'Tis a great furnace of wrath, a wide and bottomless pit, full of the fire of wrath, that you are held over in the hand of that God whose wrath is provoked and incensed as much against you as against many of the damned in hell. You hang by a slender thread, with the flames of divine wrath flashing about it, and ready every moment to singe it and burn it asunder; and you have no interest in any Mediator, and nothing to lay hold of to save yourself, nothing to keep off the flames of wrath, nothing of your own, nothing that you ever have done, nothing that you can do, to induce God to spare you one moment.

And consider here more particularly several things concerning that wrath that you are in such danger of.

1. *Whose* wrath it is. It is the wrath of the infinite God. If it were only the wrath of man, though it were of the most potent prince, it would be comparatively little to be regarded. The wrath of kings is very much dreaded, especially of absolute monarchs, that have the possessions and lives of their subjects wholly in their power, to be disposed of at their mere will. Prov. xx. 2, "The fear of a king is as the roaring of a lion: whoso provoketh him to anger sinneth against his own soul." The subject that very much enrages an arbitrary prince is liable to suffer the most extreme torments that human art can invent, or human power can inflict. But the greatest earthly potentates, in their greatest majesty and strength, and when clothed in their greatest terrors, are but feeble, despicable worms of the dust, in comparison of the great and almighty Creator and King of heaven and earth: it is but little that they can do when most enraged, and when they have exerted the utmost of their fury. All the kings of the earth before God are as grasshoppers; they are nothing, and less than nothing: both their love and their hatred is to be despised. The wrath of the great King of kings is as much more terrible than theirs, as his majesty is greater. Luke xii. 4, 5, "And I say unto you my friends, Be not afraid of them that kill the body, and after that have no more that they can do. But I will forewarn you whom you shall fear: Fear him, which after he hath killed hath power to cast into hell; yea, I say unto you, Fear him."

2. 'Tis the *fierceness* of his wrath that you are exposed to. We often read of the *fury* of God; as in Isaiah lix. 18: "According to their deeds, accordingly he will repay fury to his adversaries." So Isaiah lxvi. 15, "For, behold, the Lord will come with fire, and with his chariots like a whirlwind, to render his anger with fury, and his rebuke with flames of fire." And so in many other places. So we read of God's *fierceness*, Rev. xix. 15. There we read of "the wine-press of the fierceness and wrath of Almighty God." The words are exceeding terrible: if it had only been said, "the wrath of God," the words would have implied that which is infinitely dreadful: but 'tis not only said so, but "the fierceness and wrath of God." The fury of God! The fierceness of Jehovah! Oh, how dreadful must that be! Who can utter or conceive what such expressions carry in them! But it is not only said so, but "the fierceness and wrath of Almighty God." As though there would be a very great manifestation of his almighty power in what the fierceness of his wrath should inflict, as though omnipotence should be as it were enraged, and exerted, as men are wont to exert their strength in the fierceness of their wrath. Oh! then, what will be the consequence! What will become of the poor worm that shall suffer it! Whose hands can be strong! And whose heart endure! To what a dreadful, inexpressible, inconceivable depth of misery must the poor creature be sunk who shall be the subject of this!

Consider this, you that are here present, that yet remain in an unregenerate state. That God will execute the fierceness of his anger implies that he will inflict wrath without any pity. When God beholds the ineffable extremity of your case, and sees your torment so vastly disproportioned to your strength, and sees how your poor soul is crushed, and sinks down, as it were, into an infinite gloom;

he will have no compassion upon you, he will not forbear the executions of his wrath, or in the least lighten his hand; there shall be no moderation or mercy, nor will God then at all stay his rough wind; he will have no regard to your welfare, nor be at all careful lest you should suffer too much in any other sense, than only that you should not suffer beyond what strict justice requires: nothing shall be withheld because it is so hard for you to bear. Ezek. viii. 18, "Therefore will I also deal in fury: mine eye shall not spare, neither will I have pity: and though they cry in mine ears with a loud voice, yet will I not hear them." Now God stands ready to pity you; this is a day of mercy; you may cry now with some encouragement of obtaining mercy: but when once the day of mercy is past, your most lamentable and dolorous cries and shrieks will be in vain; you will be wholly lost and thrown away of God, as to any regard to your welfare; God will have no other use to put you to, but only to suffer misery; you shall be continued in being to no other end; for you will be a vessel of wrath fitted to destruction; and there will be no other use of this vessel, but only to be filled full of wrath: God will be so far from pitying you when you cry to him, that 'tis said he will only "laugh and mock," Prov. i. 25, 26, &c.

How awful are those words, Isaiah lxiii. 3, which are the words of the great God: "I will tread them in mine anger, and trample them in my fury; and their blood shall be sprinkled upon my garments, and I will stain all my raiment." 'Tis perhaps impossible to conceive of words that carry in them greater manifestations of these three things, viz., contempt and hatred and fierceness of indignation. If you cry to God to pity you, he will be so far from pitying you in your doleful case, or showing you the least regard or favor, that instead of that he'll only tread you under foot: and though he will know that you can't bear the weight of omnipotence treading upon you, yet he won't regard that, but he will crush you under his feet without mercy; he'll crush out your blood, and make it fly, and it shall be sprinkled on his garments, so as to stain all his raiment. He will not only hate you, but he will have you in the utmost contempt; no place shall be thought fit for you but under his feet, to be trodden down as the mire of the streets.

3. The misery you are exposed to is that which God will inflict to that end, that he might *show* what that *wrath* of *Jehovah* is. God hath had it on his heart to show to angels and men, both how excellent his love is, and also how terrible his wrath is. Sometimes earthly kings have a mind to show how terrible their wrath is, by the extreme punishments they would execute on those that provoke 'em. Nebuchadnezzar, that mighty and haughty monarch of the Chaldean empire, was willing to show his wrath when enraged with Shadrach, Meshech, and Abednego; and accordingly gave order that the burning fiery furnace should be heated seven times hotter than it was before; doubtless, it was raised to the utmost degree of fierceness that human art could raise it; but the great God is also willing to show his wrath, and magnify his awful Majesty and mighty power in the extreme sufferings of his enemies. Rom. ix. 22, "What if God, willing to show his wrath, and to make his power known, endured with much long-suffering the vessels of wrath fitted to destruction?" And seeing this is his design, and what he has determined, to show how terrible the unmixed, unrestrained wrath, the fury and fierceness of Jehovah is, he will do it to effect. There will be something accomplished and brought to pass that will be dreadful with a witness. When the great and angry God hath risen up and executed his awful vengeance on the poor sinner, and the wretch is actually suffering the infinite weight and power of his indignation, then will God call upon the whole universe to behold that awful majesty and mighty power that is to be seen in it. Isa. xxxiii. 12, 13, 14, "And the people shall be as the burnings of lime, as thorns cut up shall they be burnt in the fire. Hear, ye that are far off, what I have

done; and ye that are near, acknowledge my might. The sinners in Zion are afraid; fearfulness hath surprised the hypocrites," &c.

Thus it will be with you that are in an unconverted state, if you continue in it; the infinite might, and majesty, and terribleness, of the Omnipotent God shall be magnified upon you in the ineffable strength of your torments. You shall be tormented in the presence of the holy angels, and in the presence of the Lamb; and when you shall be in this state of suffering, the glorious inhabitants of heaven shall go forth and look on the awful spectacle, that they may see what the wrath and fierceness of the Almighty is; and when they have seen it, they will fall down and adore that great power and majesty. Isa. lxvi. 23, 24, "And it shall come to pass, that from one new moon to another, and from one sabbath to another, shall all flesh come to worship before me, saith the Lord. And they shall go forth, and look upon the carcasses of the men that have transgressed against me: for their worm shall not die, neither shall their fire be quenched; and they shall be an abhorring unto all flesh."

4. It is *everlasting* wrath. It would be dreadful to suffer this fierceness and wrath of Almighty God one moment; but you must suffer it to all eternity: there will be no end to this exquisite, horrible misery. When you look forward, you shall see a long forever, a boundless duration before you, which will swallow up your thoughts, and amaze your soul; and you will absolutely despair of ever having any deliverance, any end, any mitigation, any rest at all; you will know certainly that you must wear out long ages, millions of millions of ages, in wrestling and conflicting with this almighty, merciless vengeance; and then when you have so done, when so many ages have actually been spent by you in this manner, you will know that all is but a point to what remains. So that your punishment will indeed be infinite. Oh, who can express what the state of a soul in such circumstances is! All that we can possibly say about it gives but a very feeble, faint representation of it; it is inexpressible and inconceivable: for "who knows the power of God's anger?"

How dreadful is the state of those that are daily and hourly in danger of this great wrath and infinite misery! But this is the dismal case of every soul in this congregation that has not been born again, however moral and strict, sober and religious, they may otherwise be. Oh, that you would consider it, whether you be young or old! There is reason to think that there are many in this congregation now hearing this discourse, that will actually be the subjects of this very misery to all eternity. We know not who they are, or in what seats they sit, or what thoughts they now have. It may be they are now at ease, and hear all these things without much disturbance, and are now flattering themselves that they are not the persons, promising themselves that they shall escape. If we knew that there was one person, and but one, in the whole congregation, that was to be the subject of this misery, what an awful thing it would be to think of! If we knew who it was, what an awful sight would it be to see such a person! How might all the rest of the congregation lift up a lamentable and bitter cry over him! But alas! instead of one, how many is it likely will remember this discourse in hell! And it would be a wonder, if some that are now present should not be in hell in a very short time, before this year is out. And it would be no wonder if some persons that now sit here in some seats of this meeting-house in health, and quiet and secure, should be there before to-morrow morning. Those of you that finally continue in a natural condition, that shall keep out of hell longest, will be there in a little time! Your damnation don't slumber; it will come swiftly and, in all probability, very suddenly upon many of you. You have reason to wonder that you are not already in hell. 'Tis doubtless the case of some that heretofore you have seen and known, that never deserved hell more than you and that heretofore appeared as likely to have been now alive as you. Their case is past all hope; they are crying in extreme misery and perfect despair. But here you are in the land of the living and in the house of God, and have an opportunity to obtain salvation. What would not those poor, damned, hopeless souls give for one day's such opportunity as you now enjoy!

And now you have an extraordinary opportunity, a day wherein Christ has flung the door of mercy wide open, and stands in the door calling and crying with a loud voice to poor sinners; a day wherein many are flocking to him and pressing into the Kingdom of God. Many are daily coming from the east, west, north and south; many that were very likely in the same miserable condition that you are in are in now a happy state, with their hearts filled with love to him that has loved them and washed them from their sins in his own blood, and rejoicing in hope of the glory of God. How awful is it to be left behind at such a day! To see so many others feasting, while you are pining and perishing! To see so many rejoicing and singing for joy of heart, while you have cause to mourn for sorrow of heart and howl for vexation of spirit! How can you rest for one moment in such a condition? Are not your souls as precious as the souls of the people at Suffield, where they are flocking from day to day to Christ?

Are there not many here that have lived long in the world that are not to this day born again, and so are aliens from the commonwealth of Israel and have done nothing ever since they have lived but treasure up wrath against the day of wrath? Oh, sirs, your case in an especial manner is extremely dangerous; your guilt and hardness of heart is extremely great. Don't you see how generally persons of your years are passed over and left in the present remarkable and wonderful dispensation of God's mercy? You had need to consider yourselves and wake thoroughly out of sleep; you cannot bear the fierceness and the wrath of the infinite God.

And you that are young men and young women, will you neglect this precious season that you now enjoy, when so many others of your age are renouncing all youthful vanities and flocking to Christ? You especially have now an extraordinary opportunity; but if you neglect it, it will soon be with you as it is with those persons that spent away all the precious days of youth in sin and are now come to such a dreadful pass in blindness and hardness.

And you children that are unconverted, don't you know that you are going down to hell to bear the dreadful wrath of that God that is now angry with you every day and every night? Will you be content to be the children of the devil, when so many other children in the land are converted and are become the holy and happy children of the King of kings?

And let every one that is yet out of Christ and hanging over the pit of hell, whether they be old men and women or middle-aged or young people or little children, now hearken to the loud calls of God's word and providence. This acceptable year of the Lord that is a day of such great favor to some will doubtless be a day of as remarkable vengeance to others. Men's hearts harden and their guilt increases apace at such a day as this, if they neglect their souls. And never was there so great danger of such persons being given up to hardness of heart and blindness of mind. God seems now to be hastily gathering in his elect in all parts of the land; and probably the bigger part of adult persons that ever shall be saved will be brought in now in a little time, and that it will be as it was on that great outpouring of the Spirit upon the Jews in the Apostles' days, the election will obtain and the rest will be blinded. If this should be the case with you, you will eternally curse this day, and will curse the day that ever you was born to see such a season of the pouring out of God's Spirit, and will wish that you had died and gone to hell before you had seen it. Now undoubtedly it is as it was in the days of John the Baptist, the axe is in an extraordinary manner laid at the root of the trees, that every tree that bringeth not forth good fruit may be hewn down and cast into the fire.

Therefore let every one that is out of Christ now awake and fly from the wrath to come. The wrath of Almighty God is now undoubtedly hanging over great part of this congregation. Let every one fly out of Sodom. "*Haste and escape for your lives, look not behind you, escape to the mountain, lest ye be consumed.*"

VI

GOD'S AWFUL JUDGMENT IN THE BREAKING AND WITHERING OF THE STRONG RODS OF A COMMUNITY°

EZEK. xix. 12.—Her strong rods were broken and withered.

In order to a right understanding and improving these words, these four things must be observed and understood concerning them.

1. *Who she is* that is here represented as having had strong rods, viz., the Jewish community, here, as often elsewhere, is called the people's mother. She is here compared to a vine planted in a very fruitful soil, verse 10. The Jewish church and state is often elsewhere compared to a vine; as Psalm lxxx. 8, &c., Isai. v. 2, Jer. ii. 21, Ezek. xv., and chapter xvii. 6.

2. What is meant by *her strong rods*, viz., her wise, able, and well qualified magistrates or rulers. That the rulers or magistrates are intended is manifest by verse 11: "And she had strong rods for the sceptres of them that bare rule." And by rods that were strong, must be meant such rulers as were well qualified for magistracy, such as had great abilities and other qualifications fitting them for the business of rule. They were wont to choose a rod or staff of the strongest and hardest sort of wood that could be found, for the mace or sceptre of a prince; such a one only being counted fit for such a use: and this generally was overlaid with gold.

It is very remarkable that such a strong rod should grow out of a weak vine; but so it had been in Israel, through God's extraordinary blessing, in times past. Though the nation is spoken of here, and frequently elsewhere, as weak and helpless in itself and entirely dependent as a vine, that is the weakest of all trees, that can't support itself by its own strength, and never stands but as it leans on or hangs by something else that is stronger than itself; yet God had caused many of her sons to be strong rods, fit for sceptres; he had raised up in Israel many able and excellent princes and magistrates in days past, that had done worthily in their day.

3. It should be understood and observed what is meant by these strong rods being *broken and withered*, viz., these able and excellent rulers being removed by death. Man's dying is often compared in Scripture to the withering of the growth of the earth.

4. It should be observed *after what manner* the breaking and withering of these strong rods is here spoken of, viz., as a great and awful calamity that God had brought upon that people. 'Tis spoken of as one of the chief effects of God's fury and dreadful displeasure against them. "But she was plucked up in fury, she was cast down to the ground, and the east wind dried up her fruit; her strong rods were broken and withered, the fire hath consumed them." The great benefits she enjoyed while her strong rods remained are represented in the preceding verse: "And she had strong rods for the sceptres of them that bare rule, and her stature was exalted among the thick branches, and she appeared in her height with the multitude of her branches." And the terrible calamities that attended the breaking and withering of her strong rods, are represented in the two verses next following the text: "And now she is planted in the wilderness, in a dry and thirsty ground. And fire is gone out of a rod of her branches, which hath devoured her fruit." And in the conclusion in the next words is very

emphatically declared the worthiness of such a dispensation to be greatly lamented: "So that she hath no strong rod to be a sceptre to rule. This is a lamentation, and shall be for a lamentation."

That which I therefore observe from the words of the text to be the subject of discourse at this time, is this:

When God by death removes from a people those in place of public authority and rule that have been as strong rods, 'tis an awful judgment of God on that people, and worthy of great lamentation.

In discoursing on this proposition, I would,

I. Show what kind of rulers may fitly be called strong rods.

II. Show why the removal of such rulers from a people, by death, is to be looked upon as an awful judgment of God on that people, and is greatly to be lamented.

I. I would observe what qualifications of those who are in public authority and rule may properly give them the denomination of *strong rods.*

I. One qualification of rulers whence they may properly be denominated strong rods is *great ability for the management of public affairs.* When they that stand in place of public authority are men of great natural abilities, when they are men of uncommon strength of reason and largeness of understanding; especially when they have remarkably a genius for government, a peculiar turn of mind fitting them to gain an extraordinary understanding in things of that nature, giving ability, in an especial manner, for insight into the mysteries of government, and discerning those things wherein the public welfare or calamity consists and the proper means to avoid the one and promote the other; an extraordinary talent at distinguishing what is right and just from that which is wrong and unequal, and to see through the false colors with which injustice is often disguised, and unravel the false, subtle arguments and cunning sophistry that is often made use of to defend iniquity; and when they have not only great natural abilities in these respects, but when their abilities and talents have been improved by study, learning, observation and experience; and when by these means they have obtained great actual knowledge; when they have acquired great skill in public affairs and things requisite to be known in order to their wise, prudent, and effectual management; when they have obtained a great understanding of men and things, a great knowledge of human nature and of the way of accommodating themselves to it, so as most effectually to influence it to wise purposes; when they have obtained a very extensive knowledge of men with whom they are concerned in the management of public affairs, either those that have a joint concern in government or those that are to be governed; and when they have also obtained a very full and particular understanding of the state and circumstances of the country or people that they have the care of, and know well their laws and constitution and what their circumstances require; and likewise have a great knowledge of the people of neighbor nations, states, or provinces with whom they have occasion to be concerned in the management of public affairs committed to them; these things all contribute to the rendering those that are in authority fit to be denominated strong rods.

2. When they have not only great understanding but *largeness of heart and a greatness and nobleness of disposition*, this is another qualification that belongs to the character of a strong rod.

Those that are by divine Providence set in places of public authority and rule are called *gods*, and *sons of the Most High*, Psalm lxxxii. 6. And therefore 'tis peculiarly unbecoming them to be of a mean spirit, a disposition that will admit of their doing those things that are sordid and vile; as when they are persons of a narrow, private spirit, that may be found in little tricks and intrigues to promote their private interest, will shamefully defile their hands to gain a few pounds, are not ashamed to nip and bite others, grind the faces of the poor and screw upon their neighbors, and will take advantage of their authority or commission to line their own pockets with what is fraudulently taken or withheld from others. When a man in authority is of such a mean spirit, it weakens his authority and makes him justly contemptible in the eyes of men and is utterly inconsistent with his being a *strong rod*.

But on the contrary, it greatly establishes his authority, and causes others to stand in awe of him, when they see him to be a man of greatness of mind, one that abhors those things that are mean and sordid, and not capable of a compliance with them; one that is of a public spirit, and not of a private, narrow disposition; a man of honor, and not a man of mean artifice and clandestine management for filthy lucre, and one that abhors trifling and impertinence, or to waste away his time, that should be spent in the service of God, his king, or his country, in vain amusements and diversions and in the pursuit of the gratifications of sensual appetites; as God charges the rulers in Israel, that pretended to be their great and mighty men, with being mighty to drink wine and men of strength to mingle strong drink. There don't seem to be any reference to their being men of strong heads and able to bear a great deal of strong drink, as some have supposed. There is a severe sarcasm in the words; for the prophet is speaking of the great men, princes and judges in Israel (as appears by the verse next following), which should be mighty men, strong rods, men of eminent qualifications, excelling in nobleness of spirit, of glorious strength and fortitude of mind; but instead of that, they were mighty or eminent for nothing but gluttony and drunkenness.

3. When those that are in authority are endowed with much of *a spirit of government*, this is another thing that entitles them to the denomination of strong rods. When they not only are men of great understanding and wisdom in affairs that appertain to government, but have also a peculiar talent at using their knowledge and exerting themselves in this great and important business, according to their great understanding in it; when they are men of eminent fortitude and are not afraid of the faces of men, are not afraid to do the part that properly belongs to them as rulers, though they meet with great opposition, and the spirits of men are greatly irritated by it; when they have a spirit of resolution and activity, so as to keep the wheels of government in proper motion and to cause judgment and justice to run down as a mighty stream; when they have not only a great knowledge of government and the things that belong to it in the theory, but it is, as it were, natural to them to apply the various powers and faculties with which God has endowed them, and the knowledge they have obtained by study and observation, to that business, so as to perform it most advantageously and effectually.

4. *Stability and firmness of integrity, fidelity and piety in the exercise of authority* is another thing that greatly contributes to, and is very essential in, the character of a strong rod.

When he that is in authority is not only a man of strong reason and great discerning to know what is just, but is a man of strict integrity and righteousness, is firm and immovable in the execution of justice and judgment; and when he is not only a man of great ability to bear down vice and immorality, but has a disposition agreeable to such ability; is one that has a strong aversion to wickedness and is disposed to use the power God has put into his hands to suppress it; and is one that not only opposes vice by his authority, but by his example; when he is one of inflexible fidelity, will be faithful to God whose minister he is to his people for good, is immovable in his regard to his supreme authority, his commands and his glory, and will be faithful to his king and country; will not be induced by the many temptations that attend the business of men in public authority basely to betray his trust; will not consent to do what he thinks not to be for the public good for his own gain or advancement, or any private interest; is one that is well principled, and is firm in acting agreeably to his principles, and will not be prevailed with to do otherwise through fear or favor, to follow a multitude, or to maintain his interest in any on whom he depends for the honor or profit of his place, whether it be prince or people; and is also one of that strength of mind, whereby he rules his own spirit,—these things do very eminently contribute to a ruler's title to the denomination of a *strong rod*.

5. And lastly, it also contributes to the strength of a man in authority by which he may be denominated a *strong rod*, when he is in *such circumstances as give him advantage* for the exercise of his strength for the public good; as his being a person of honorable descent, of a distinguished education, his being a man of estate, one that is advanced in years, one that has long been in authority, so that it is become, as it were, natural for the people to pay him deference, to reverence him, to be influenced and governed by him and submit to his authority; his being extensively known and much honored and regarded abroad; his being one of a good presence, majesty of countenance, decency of behavior, becoming one in authority; of forcible speech, &c. These things add to his strength and increase his ability and advantage to serve his generation in the place of a ruler, and therefore in some respect serve to render him one that is the more fitly and eminently called a *strong rod*.

I now proceed,

II. To show that when such strong rods are broken and withered by death, 'tis an awful judgment of God on the people that are deprived of them and worthy of great lamentation.

And that on two accounts:

1. By reason of the many *positive benefits* and blessings to a people that such rulers are the instruments of.

Almost all the prosperity of a public society and civil community does, under God, depend on their rulers. They are like the main springs or wheels in a machine that keep every part in their due motion, and are in the body politic, as the vitals in the body natural, and as the pillars and foundation in a building. Civil rulers are called "the foundations of the earth," Psalm lxxxii. 5, and xi. 3.

The prosperity of a people depends more on their rulers than is commonly imagined. As they have the public society under their care and power, so they have advantage to promote the public interest every way; and if they are such rulers as have been spoken of, they are some of the greatest blessings to the public. Their influence has a tendency to promote their wealth and cause their temporal possessions and blessings to abound: and to promote virtue amongst them, and so to unite them one to another in peace and mutual benevolence, and make them happy in society, each one the instrument of his neighbor's quietness, comfort and prosperity; and by these means to advance their reputation and honor in the world; and which is much more, to promote their spiritual and eternal happiness. Therefore, the wise man says, Eccles. x. 17, "Blessed art thou, O land, when thy king is the son of nobles."

We have a remarkable instance and evidence of the happy and great influence of such a strong rod as has been described to promote the universal prosperity of a people in the history of the reign of Solomon, though many of the people were uneasy under his government, and thought him too rigorous in his administration (see 1 Kings xii. 4). "Judah and Israel dwelt safely, every man under his vine and under his fig-tree, from Dan even to Beersheba, all the days of Solomon," 1 Kings iv. 25. "And he made silver to be among them as stones for abundance," chap x. 27. "And Judah and Israel were many, eating and drinking and making merry," . The queen of Sheba admired and was greatly affected with the happiness of the people under the government of such a strong rod: 1 Kings x. 8, 9, says she, "Happy are thy men, happy are these thy servants which stand continually before thee, and that hear thy wisdom. Blessed be the Lord thy God which delighted in thee, to set thee on the throne of Israel; because the Lord loved Israel forever, therefore made he thee king, to do judgment and justice."

The flourishing state of the kingdom of Judah, while they had strong rods for the sceptres of them that bare rule, is taken notice of in our context: "Her stature was exalted among the thick branches, and she appeared in her height with the multitude of her branches."

Such rulers are eminently the ministers of God to his people for good: they are great gifts of the Most High to a people and blessed tokens of his favor and vehicles of his goodness to them, and therein images of his own Son, the grand medium of all God's goodness to fallen mankind: and therefore, all of them are called *sons of the Most High*. All civil rulers, if they are, as they ought to be, such strong rods as have been described, will be like the Son of the Most High, vehicles of good to mankind, and like him, will be as the light of the morning when the sun riseth, even a morning without clouds, as the tender grass springeth out of the earth, by clear shining after rain. And therefore, when a people are bereaved of them, they sustain an unspeakable loss and are the subjects of a judgment of God that is greatly to be lamented.

2. On account of the *great calamities* such rulers are *a defence from*. Innumerable are the grievous and fatal calamities which public societies are exposed to in this evil world, which they can have no defence from without order and authority. If a people are without government, they are like a city broken down and without walls, encompassed on every side by enemies and become unavoidably subject to all manner of confusion and misery.

Government is necessary to *defend communities from miseries from within themselves*, from the prevalence of intestine discord, mutual injustice and violence; the members of the society continually making a prey one of another, without any defence one from another. Rulers are the heads of union in public societies, that hold the parts together; without which nothing else is to be expected than that the members of the society will be continually divided against themselves, every one acting the part of an enemy to his neighbor, every one's hand against every man and every man's hand against him; going on in remediless and endless broils and jarring till the society be utterly dissolved and broken in pieces and life itself, in the neighborhood of our fellow creatures, becomes miserable and intolerable.

We may see the need of government in societies by what is visible in families, those lesser societies of which all public societies are constituted. How miserable would these little societies be, if all were left to themselves, without any authority or superiority in one above another or any head of union and influence among them? We may be convinced by what we see of the lamentable consequences of the want of a proper exercise of authority and maintenance of government in families that yet are not absolutely without all authority. No less need is there of government in public societies, but much more, as they are larger. A very few may possibly, without any government, act by concert, so as to concur in what shall be for the welfare of the whole; but this is not to be expected among a multitude, constituted of many thousands, of a great variety of tempers, and different interests.

As government is absolutely necessary, so there is a necessity of *strong rods* in order to it: the business being such as requires persons so qualified: no other being sufficient for, or well capable of the government of, public societies: and therefore, those public societies are miserable that have not such strong rods for sceptres to rule: Eccles. x. 16, "Woe to thee, O land, when thy king is a child."

As government, and strong rods for the exercise of it, are necessary to preserve public societies from dreadful and fatal calamities arising from among themselves; so no less requisite are they to *defend the community from foreign enemies*. As they are like the pillars of a building, so they are also like the walls and bulwarks of a city: they are under God the main strength of a people in a time of war and the chief instruments of their preservation, safety and rest. This is signified in a very lively manner in the words that are used by the Jewish community in her Lamentations to express the expectations she had from her princes: Lam. iv. 29, "The breath of our nostrils, the anointed of the Lord, was taken in their pits, of whom we said, Under his shadow we shall live among the heathen." In this respect also such strong rods are sons of the Most High and images or resemblances of the Son of God, viz., as they are their saviours from their enemies; as the judges that God raised up of old in Israel are called, Nehem. ix. 27: "Therefore thou deliveredst them into the hand of their enemies, who vexed them: and in the time of their trouble, when they cried unto thee, thou heardest them from heaven; and according to thy manifold mercies thou gavest them saviours, who saved them out of the hand of their enemies."

Thus both the prosperity and safety of a people under God, depends on such rulers as are *strong rods*. While they enjoy such blessings, they are wont to be like a vine planted in a fruitful soil, with her stature exalted among the thick branches, appearing in her height with the multitude of her branches; but when they have no strong rod to be a sceptre to rule, they are like a vine planted in a wilderness that is exposed to be plucked up and cast down to the ground, to have her fruit dried up with the east wind, and to have fire coming out of her own branches to devour her fruit.

On these accounts, when a people's strong rods are broken and withered, 'tis an awful judgment of God on that people, and worthy of great lamentation: as when King Josiah (who was doubtless one of the strong rods referred to in the text) was dead, the people made great lamentation for him, 2 Chron. xxxv. 24, 25: "And they brought him to Jerusalem, and he died, and was buried in one of the sepulchres of his fathers. And all Judah and Jerusalem mourned for Josiah. And Jeremiah lamented for

Josiah: and all the singing men and the singing women spake of Josiah in their lamentations to this day, and made them an ordinance in Israel: and, behold, they are written in the Lamentations."

APPLICATION

I come now to apply these things to our own case, under the late awful frown of divine Providence upon us in removing by death that honorable person in public rule and authority, an inhabitant of this town and belonging to this congregation and church, who died at Boston the last Lord's day.

He was eminently a *strong rod* in the forementioned respects. As to his natural abilities, strength of reason, greatness and clearness of discerning and depth of penetration, he was one of the first rank: it may be doubted whether he has left his superior in these respects in these parts of the world. He was a man of a truly great genius, and his genius was peculiarly fitted for the understanding and managing of public affairs.

And as his natural capacity was great, so was the knowledge that he had acquired, his understanding being greatly improved by close application of mind to those things he was called to be concerned in, and by a very exact observation of them and long experience in them. He had indeed a great insight into the nature of public societies, the mysteries of government and the affairs of peace and war: he had a discerning that very few have of the things wherein the public weal consists, and what those things are that do expose public societies, and of the proper means to avoid the latter and promote the former. He was quick in his discerning, in that in most cases, especially such as belonged to his proper business, he at first sight would see further than most men when they had done their best; but yet he had a wonderful faculty of improving his own thoughts by meditation, and carrying his views a greater and greater length by long and close application of mind. He had an extraordinary ability to distinguish right and wrong in the midst of intricacies and circumstances that tended to perplex and darken the case: he was able to weigh things, as it were, in a balance, and to distinguish those things that were solid and weighty from those that had only a fair show without substance, which he evidently discovered in his accurate, clear and plain way of stating and committing causes to a jury, from the bench, as by others hath been observed. He wonderfully distinguished truth from falsehood, and the most labored cases seemed always to lie clear in his mind, his ideas properly ranged—and he had a talent of communicating them to every one's understanding, beyond almost any one; and if any were misguided, it was not because truth and falsehood, right and wrong, were not well distinguished.

He was probably one of the ablest politicians that ever New England bred: he had a very uncommon insight into human nature, and a marvellous ability to penetrate into the particular tempers and dispositions of such as he had to deal with, and to discern the fittest way of treating them, so as most effectually to influence them to any good and wise purpose.

And never perhaps was there a person that had a more extensive and thorough knowledge of the state of this land and its public affairs, and of persons that were jointly concerned in them: he knew this people and their circumstances, and what their circumstances required: he discerned the diseases of this body, and what were the proper remedies, as an able and masterly physician. He had a great acquaintance with the neighboring colonies, and also the neighbor nations on this continent, with whom we are concerned in our public affairs: he had a far greater knowledge than any other person in the land of the several nations of Indians in these northern parts of America, their tempers, manners and the proper way of treating them, and was more extensively known by them than any other person in the country: and no other person in authority in this province had such an acquaintance with the people and country of Canada, the land of our enemies, as he.

He was exceeding far from a disposition and forwardness to intermeddle with other people's business; but as to what belonged to the offices he sustained and the important affairs that he had the care of, he had a great understanding of what belonged to them. I have often been surprised at the length of his reach, and what I have seen of his ability to foresee and determine the consequences of things, even at a great distance, and quite beyond the sight of other men. He was not wavering and unsteady in his opinion: his manner was never to pass a judgment rashly, but was wont first thoroughly to deliberate and weigh an affair; and in this, notwithstanding his great abilities, he was glad to improve   the help of conversation and discourse with others, and often spake of the great advantage he found by it; but when, on mature consideration, he had settled his judgment, he was not easily turned from it by false colors and plausible pretences and appearances.

And besides his knowledge of things belonging to his particular calling as a ruler, he had also a great degree of understanding in things belonging to his general calling as a Christian. He was no inconsiderable divine. He was a wise casuist, as I know by the great help I have found from time to time by his judgment and advice in cases of conscience wherein I have consulted him: and indeed I scarce knew the divine that I ever found more able to help and enlighten the mind in such cases than he. And he had no small degree of knowledge in things pertaining to experimental religion; but was wont to discourse on such subjects, not only with accurate doctrinal distinctions, but as one intimately and feelingly acquainted with these things.

He was not only great in speculative knowledge, but his knowledge was practical; such as tended to a wise conduct in the affairs, business and duties of life; so as properly to have the denomination of wisdom, and so as properly and eminently to invest him with the character of a wise man. And he was not only eminently wise and prudent in his own conduct, but was one of the ablest and wisest counsellors of others in any difficult affair.

The greatness and honorableness of his disposition was answerable to the largeness of his understanding. He was naturally of a great mind. In this respect he was truly the *son of nobles*. He greatly abhorred things which were mean and sordid, and seemed to be incapable of a compliance with them. How far was he from trifling and impertinence in his conversation! How far from a busy, meddling disposition! How far from any sly and clandestine management to fill his pockets with what was fraudulently withheld or violently squeezed from the laborer, soldier or inferior officer! How far from taking advantage from his commission or authority or any superior power he had in his hands, or the ignorance, dependence or necessities of others, to add to his own gains with what property belonged to them, and with what they might justly expect as a proper reward for any of their services! How far was he from secretly taking bribes offered to induce him to favor any man in his cause, or by his power or interest to promote his being advanced to any place of public trust, honor or profit! How greatly did he abhor lying and prevaricating! And how immovably steadfast was he to exact truth! His hatred of those things that were mean and sordid was so apparent and well known, that it was evident that men dreaded to appear in any thing of that nature in his presence.

He was a man remarkably of a public spirit, a true lover of his country and greatly abhorred the sacrificing the public welfare to private interest.

He was very eminently endowed with a spirit of government. The God of nature seemed to have formed him for government, as though he had been made on purpose, and cast into a mould by which he should be every way fitted for the business of a man in public authority. Such a behavior and conduct was natural to him as tended to maintain his authority and possess others with awe and reverence, and to enforce and render effectual what he said and did in the exercise of his authority. He did not *bear the sword in vain*: he was truly a *terror to evil doers*. What I saw in him often put me in mind of that saying of the wise man, Prov. xx. 8, "The king that sitteth on the throne of judgment scattereth away all evil with his eyes." He was one that was not afraid of the faces of men; and every one knew that it was in vain to attempt to deter him from doing what, on mature consideration, he had determined he ought to do. Every thing in him was great and becoming a man in his public station. Perhaps never was there a man that appeared in New England to whom the denomination of a *great man* did more properly belong.

But though he was one that was great among men, exalted above others in abilities and greatness of mind and in place of rule, and feared not the faces of men, yet he feared God. He was strictly conscientious in his conduct, both in public and private. I never knew the man that seemed more steadfastly and immovably to act by principle and according to rules and maxims, established and settled in his mind by the dictates of his judgment and conscience. He was a man of strict justice and fidelity. Faithfulness was eminently his character. Some of his greatest opponents that have been of the contrary party to him in public affairs, yet have openly acknowledged this of him, that he was a faithful man. He was remarkably faithful in his public trusts: he would not basely betray his trust, from fear or favor. It was in vain to expect it, however men might oppose him or neglect him, and how great soever they were. Nor would he neglect the public interest, wherein committed to him, for the sake of his own ease, but diligently and laboriously watched and labored for it night and day. And he was faithful in private affairs as well as public: he was a most faithful friend, faithful to any one that in any case asked his counsel; and his fidelity might be depended on in whatever affair he undertook for any of his neighbors.

He was a noted instance of the virtue of temperance, unalterable in it, in all places, in all companies, and in the midst of all temptations.

Though he was a man of a great spirit, yet he had a remarkable government of his spirit; and excelled in the government of his tongue. In the midst of all provocations he met with, among the multitudes he had to deal with, and the great multiplicity of perplexing affairs in which he was concerned, and all the opposition and reproaches he was at any time the subject of; yet what was there that ever proceeded out of his mouth that his enemies could lay hold of? No profane language, no vain, rash, unseemly and unchristian speeches. If at any time he expressed himself with great warmth and vigor, it seemed to be from principle and determination of his judgment, rather than from passion. When he expressed himself strongly and with vehemence, those that were acquainted with him, and well observed him from time to time, might evidently see it was done in consequence of thought and judgment, weighing the circumstances and consequences of things.

The calmness and steadiness of his behavior in private, particularly in his family, appeared remarkable and exemplary to those who had most opportunity to observe it.

He was thoroughly established in those religious principles and doctrines of the first fathers of New England, usually called the *doctrines of grace*, and had a great detestation of the opposite errors of the present fashionable divinity, as very contrary to the word of God and the experience of every true Christian. And as he was a friend to truth, so he was a friend to vital piety and the power of godliness, and ever countenanced and favored it on all occasions.

He abhorred profaneness, and was a person of a serious and decent spirit, and ever treated sacred things with reverence. He was exemplary for his decent attendance on the public worship of God. Who ever saw him irreverently and indecently lolling and laying down his head to sleep, or gazing and staring about the meeting-house in time of divine service? And as he was able (as was before observed) to discourse very understandingly of experimental religion, so to some persons with whom he was very intimate, he gave intimations sufficiently plain, while conversing of these things, that they were matters of his own experience. And some serious persons in civil authority that have ordinarily differed from him in matters of government, yet, on some occasional close conversation with him on things of religion, have manifested a high opinion of him as to real experimental piety.

As he was known to be a serious person, and an enemy to a profane or vain conversation, so he was feared on that account by great and small. When he was in the room, only his presence was sufficient to maintain decency; though many were there that were accounted gentlemen and great men, who otherwise were disposed to take a much greater freedom in their talk and behavior than they dared to do in his presence.

He was not unmindful of death, nor insensible of his own frailty, nor did death come unexpected to him. For some years past he has spoken much to some persons of dying and going into the eternal world, signifying that he did not expect to continue long here.

Added to all these things that have been mentioned to render him eminently a *strong rod*, he was attended with many circumstances which tended to give him advantage for the exerting of his strength for the public good. He was honorably descended, was a man of considerable substance, had been long in authority, was extensively known and honored abroad, was high in the esteem of the many tribes of Indians in the neighborhood of the British colonies, and so had great influence upon them above any other man in New England; God had endowed him with a comely presence and majesty of countenance, becoming the great qualities of his mind and the place in which God had set him.

In the exercise of these qualities and endowments, under these advantages, he has been, as it were, a father to this part of the land, on whom the whole county had, under God, its dependence in all its public affairs, and especially since the beginning of the present war.° How much the weight of all the warlike concerns of the county (which above any part of the land lies exposed to the enemy) has lain on his shoulders, and how he has been the spring of all motion and the doer of every thing that has been done, and how wisely and faithfully he has conducted these affairs, I need not inform this congregation. You well know that he took care of the county as a father of a family of children, not neglecting men's lives and making light of their blood; but with great diligence, vigilance and prudence applying himself continually to the proper means of our safety and welfare. And especially has this his native town, where he has dwelt from his infancy, reaped the benefit of his happy influence: his wisdom has been, under God, very much our guide, and his authority our support and strength, and he has been a great honor to Northampton and ornament to our church.

He continued in full capacity of usefulness while he lived; he was indeed considerably advanced in years, but his powers of mind were not sensibly abated, and his strength of body was not so impaired but that he was able to go long journeys, in extreme heat and cold, and in a short time.

But now this "strong rod is broken and withered," and surely the judgment of God therein is very awful, and the dispensation that which may well be for a lamentation. Probably we shall be more sensible of the worth and importance of such a strong rod by the want of it. The awful voice of God in this providence is worthy to be attended to by this whole province, and especially by the people of this county, but in a more peculiar manner by us of this town. We have now this testimony of the divine displeasure added to all the other dark clouds God has lately brought over us, and his awful frowns upon us. 'Tis a dispensation, on many accounts, greatly calling for our humiliation and fear before God; an awful manifestation of his supreme, universal and absolute dominion, calling us to adore the divine sovereignty and tremble at the presence of this great God. And it is a lively instance of human frailty and mortality. We see how that none are out of the reach of death, that no greatness, no authority, no wisdom and sagacity, no honorableness of person or station, no degree of valuableness and importance exempts from the stroke of death. This is therefore a loud and solemn warning to all sorts to prepare for their departure hence.

And the memory of this person who is now gone, who was made so great a blessing while he lived, should engage us to show respect and kindness to his family. This we should do both out of respect to him and to his father, your former eminent pastor, who in his day was, in a remarkable manner, a father to this part of the land in spirituals, and especially to this town, as this his son has been in temporals.—God greatly resented it, when the children of Israel did not show kindness to the house of Jerubbaal that had been made an instrument of so much good to them: Judges viii. 35, "Neither showed they kindness to the house of Jerrubbaal, according to all the good which he had showed unto Israel."

VII

A FAREWELL SERMON°

2 COR. i. 14.—As also you have acknowledged us in part, that we are your rejoicing, even as ye also are ours in the day of the Lord Jesus.

The apostle, in the preceding part of the chapter, declares what great troubles he met with in the course of his ministry. In the text and two foregoing verses, he declares what were his comforts and supports under the troubles he met with. There are four things in particular.

1. That he had approved himself to his own conscience, verse 12: "For our own rejoicing is this, the testimony of our conscience, that in simplicity and godly sincerity, not with fleshly wisdom, but by the grace of God, we have had our conversation in the world, and more abundantly to you-ward."

2. Another thing he speaks of as matter of comfort is, that as he had approved himself to his own conscience, so he had also to the consciences of his hearers, the Corinthians, whom he now wrote to, and that they should approve of him at the day of judgment.

3. The hope he had of seeing the blessed fruit of his labors and sufferings in the ministry, in their happiness and glory, in that great day of accounts.

4. That, in his ministry among the Corinthians, he had approved himself to his Judge, who would approve and reward his faithfulness in that day.

These three last particulars are signified in my text and the preceding verse; and, indeed, all the four are implied in the text. 'Tis implied that the Corinthians had acknowledged him as their spiritual father and as one that had been faithful among them, and as the means of their future joy and glory at the day of judgment, and one whom they should then see, and have a joyful meeting with as such. 'Tis implied, that the apostle expected at that time to have a joyful meeting with them before the Judge, and with joy to behold their glory, as the fruit of his labors; and so they would be his rejoicing. 'Tis implied also that he then expected to be approved of the great Judge, when he and they should meet together before him; and that he would then acknowledge his fidelity, and that this had been the means of their glory; and that thus he would, as it were, give them to him as his crown of rejoicing. But this the apostle could not hope for, unless he had the testimony of his own conscience in his favor. And therefore the words do imply, in the strongest manner, that he had approved himself to his own conscience.

There is one thing implied in each of these particulars, and in every part of the text, which is that point I shall make the subject of my present discourse, viz.:

DOCT

Ministers, and the people that are under their care, must meet one another before Christ's tribunal at the day of judgment.

Ministers, and the people that have been under their care, must be parted in this world, how well soever they have been united: if they are not separated before, they must be parted by death; and they may be separated while life is continued. We live in a world of change, where nothing is certain or stable; and where a little time, a few revolutions of the sun bring to pass strange things, surprising alterations, in particular persons, in families, in towns and churches, in countries and nations. It often happens, that those who seem most united, in a little time are most disunited, and at the greatest distance. Thus ministers and people, between whom there has been the greatest mutual regard and strictest union, may not only differ in their judgments, and be alienated in affection, but one may rend from the other, and all relation between them be dissolved; the minister may be removed to a distant place, and they may never have any more to do with one another in this world. But if it be so, there is one meeting more that they must have, and that is in the last great day of accounts.

Here I would show,

I. In what manner ministers, and the people who have been under their care, shall meet one another at the day of judgment.

II. For what purposes.

III. For what reasons God has so ordered it, that ministers and their people shall then meet together in such a manner, and for such purposes.

I. I would show, in some particulars, in what manner ministers, and the people who have been under their care, shall meet one another at the day of judgment. Concerning this I would observe two things in general.

1. That they shall not then meet only as all mankind must then meet, but there will be something peculiar in the manner of their meeting.

2. That their meeting together at that time shall be very different from what used to be in the house of God in this world.

1. They shall not meet at that day as all the world must then meet together. I would observe a difference in two things.

(1) As to a clear actual view, and distinct knowledge and notice of each other.

Although the whole world will be then present, all mankind of all generations gathered in one vast assembly, with all of the angelic nature, both elect and fallen angels; yet we need not suppose that every one will have a distinct and particular knowledge of each individual of the whole assembled multitude, which will undoubtedly consist of many millions of millions. Though 'tis probable that men's capacities will be much greater than in the present state, yet they will not be infinite; though their understanding and comprehension will be vastly extended, yet men will not be deified. There will probably be a very enlarged view that particular persons will have of various parts and members of that vast assembly, and so of the proceedings of that great day; but yet it must needs be, that according to the nature of finite minds, some persons and some things at that day shall fall more under the notice of particular persons than others; and this (as we may well suppose) according as they shall have a nearer concern with some than others, in the transactions of the day. There will be special reason why those who have had special concerns together in this world, in their state of probation, and whose mutual affairs will be then to be tried and judged, should especially be set in one another's view. Thus we may suppose that rulers and subjects, earthly judges and those whom they have judged, neighbors who have had mutual converse, dealings and contests, heads of families and their children and servants, shall then meet, and in a peculiar distinction be set together. And especially will it be thus with ministers and their people. 'Tis evident by the text that these shall be in each other's view, shall distinctly know each other, and shall have particular notice one of another at that time.

(2) They shall meet together, as having a special concern one with another in the great transactions of that day.

Although they shall meet the whole world at that time, yet they will not have any immediate and particular concern with all. Yea, the far greater part of those who shall then be gathered together, will be such as they have had no intercourse with in their state of probation, and so will have no mutual concerns to be judged of. But as to ministers, and the people that have been under their care, they will be such as have had much immediate concern one with another, in matters of the greatest moment, that ever mankind have to do one with another in. Therefore they especially must meet and be brought together before the judge, as having special concern one with another in the design and business of that great day of accounts.

Thus their meeting, as to the manner of it, will be diverse from the meeting of mankind in general.

2. Their meeting at the day of judgment will be very diverse from their meetings one with another in this world.

Ministers and their people, while their relation continues, often meet together in this world. They are wont to meet from Sabbath to Sabbath, and at other times, for the public worship of God, and administration of ordinances, and the solemn services of God's house. And besides these meetings, they have also occasions to meet for the determining and managing their ecclesiastical affairs, for the exercise of church discipline, and the settling and adjusting those things which concern the purity and good order of public administrations. But their meeting at the day of judgment will be exceeding diverse, in its manner and circumstance, from any such meetings and interviews as they have one with another in the present state. I would observe how, in a few particulars.

(1) Now they meet together in a preparatory mutable state, but then in an unchangeable state.

Now sinners in the congregation meet their minister in a state wherein they are capable of a saving change, capable of being turned, through God's blessing on the ministrations and labors of their pastor, from the power of Satan unto God; and being brought out of a state of guilt, condemnation and wrath, to a state of peace and favor with God, to the enjoyment of the privileges of his children, and a title to their eternal inheritance. And saints now meet their minister with great remains of corruption, and sometimes under great spiritual difficulties and affliction: and therefore are yet the proper subjects of means of an happy alteration of their state, consisting in a greater freedom from these things, which they have reason to hope for in the way of an attendance on ordinances, and of which God is pleased commonly to make his ministers the instruments. And ministers and their people now meet in order to the bringing to pass such happy changes; they are the great benefits sought in their solemn meetings in this world.

But when they shall meet together at the day of judgment, it will be far otherwise. They will not then meet in order to the use of means for the bringing to effect any such changes; for they will all meet in an unchangeable state. Sinners will be in an unchangeable state: they who then shall be under the guilt and power of sin, and have the wrath of God abiding on them, shall be beyond all remedy or possibility of change, and shall meet their ministers without any hopes of relief or remedy, or getting any good by their means. And as for the saints, they will be already perfectly delivered from all their before remaining corruption, temptation, and calamities of every kind, and set forever out of their reach; and no deliverance, no happy alteration, will remain to be accomplished in the way of the use of means of grace, under the administrations of ministers. It will then be pronounced, "He that is unjust, let him be unjust still; and he that is filthy, let him be filthy still; and he that is righteous, let him be righteous still; and he that is holy, let him be holy still."

(2) Then they shall meet together in a state of clear, certain and infallible light.

Ministers are set as guides and teachers, and are represented in Scripture as lights set up in the churches; and in the present state meet their people from time to time in order to instruct and enlighten them, to correct their mistakes, and to be a voice behind them, when they turn aside to the right hand or to the left, saying, "This is the way, walk in it;" to evince and confirm the truth by exhibiting the proper evidences of it, and to refute errors and corrupt opinions, to convince the erroneous and establish the doubting. But when Christ shall come to judgment, every error and false opinion shall be detected; all deceit and illusion shall vanish away before the light of that day, as the darkness of the night vanishes at the appearance of the rising sun; and every doctrine of the word of God shall then appear in full evidence, and none shall remain unconvinced; all shall know the truth with the greatest certainty, and there shall be no mistakes to rectify.

Now ministers and their people may disagree in their judgments concerning some matters of religion, and may sometimes meet to confer together concerning those things wherein they differ, and to hear the reasons that may be offered on one side and the other; and all may be ineffectual as to any conviction of the truth: they may meet and part again, no more agreed than before; and that side which was in the wrong may remain so still; sometimes the meetings of ministers with their people in such a case of disagreeing sentiments are attended with unhappy debate and controversy, managed with much prejudice and want of candor; not tending to light and conviction, but rather to confirm and increase darkness, and establish opposition to the truth and alienation of affection one from another. But when they shall hereafter meet together, at the day of judgment, before the tribunal of the great Judge, the mind and will of Christ will be made known; and there shall no longer be any debate or difference of opinions; the evidence of the truth shall appear beyond all dispute, and all controversies shall be finally and forever decided.

Now ministers meet their people in order to enlighten and awaken the consciences of sinners: setting before them the great evil and danger of sin, the strictness of God's law, their own wickedness of heart and practice, the great guilt they are under, the wrath that abides upon them, and their impotence, blindness, poverty, and helpless and undone condition: but all is often in vain; they remain still, notwithstanding all their ministers can say, stupid and unawakened, and their consciences unconvinced. But it will not be so at their last meeting at the day of judgment; sinners, when they shall meet their minister before their great Judge, will not meet him with a stupid conscience: they will then be fully convinced of the truth of those things which they formerly heard from him, concerning the greatness and terrible majesty of God, his holiness, and hatred of sin, and his awful justice in punishing it, the strictness of his law, and the dreadfulness and truth of his threatenings, and their own unspeakable guilt and misery: and they shall never more be insensible of these things: the eyes of conscience will now be fully enlightened, and never shall be blinded again: the mouth of conscience shall now be opened, and never shall be shut any more.

Now ministers meet with their people, in public and private, in order to enlighten them concerning the state of their souls; to open and apply the rules of God's word to them, in order to their searching their own hearts, and discerning the state that they are in. But now ministers have no infallible discerning of the state of the souls of their own people; and the most skilful of them are liable to mistakes, and often are mistaken in things of this nature. Nor are the people able certainly to know the state of their minister, or one another's state; very often those pass among them for saints, and it may be eminent saints, that are grand hypocrites; and on the other hand, those are sometimes censured, or hardly received into their charity, that are indeed some of God's jewels. And nothing is more common than for men to be mistaken concerning their own state: many that are abominable to God, and the children of his wrath, think highly of themselves, as his precious saints and dear children. Yea, there is reason to think that often some that are most bold in their confidence of their safe and happy state, and think themselves not only true saints, but the most eminent saints in the congregation, are in a peculiar manner a smoke in God's nose. And thus it undoubtedly often is in those congregations where the word of God is most faithfully dispensed, notwithstanding all that ministers can say in their clearest explications and most searching applications of the doctrines and rules of God's word to the souls of their hearers, in their meetings one with another. But in the day of judgment they shall have another sort of meeting; then the secrets of every heart shall be made manifest, and every man's state shall be perfectly known: 1 Cor. iv. 5, "Therefore, judge nothing before the time, until the Lord come, who will both bring to light the hidden things of darkness, and will make manifest the counsels of the hearts: and then shall every man have praise of God." Then none shall be deceived concerning his own state, nor shall be any more in doubt about it. There shall be an eternal end to all the ill conceit and vain hopes of deluded hypocrites, and all the doubts and fears of sincere Christians. And then shall all know the state of one another's souls: the people shall know whether their minister has been sincere and faithful, and the ministers shall know the state of every one of their people, and to whom the word and ordinances of God have been a savor of life unto life, and to whom a savor of death unto death.

Now in this present state it often happens that when ministers and people meet together to debate and manage their ecclesiastical affairs, especially in a state of controversy, they are ready to judge and censure one another with regard to each other's views and designs, and the principles and ends that each is influenced by; and are greatly mistaken in their judgment, and wrong one another with regard to each other's views and designs and the principles and ends that each is influenced by, and are greatly mistaken in their judgment, and wrong one another in their censures. But at that future meeting, things will be set in a true and perfect light, and the principles and aims that every one has acted from shall be certainly known; and there will be an end to all errors of this kind, and all unrighteous censures.

(3) In this world, ministers and their people often meet together to hear of and wait upon an unseen Lord; but at the day of judgment they shall meet in his most immediate and visible presence.

Ministers, who now often meet their people to preach to 'em the King eternal, immortal, and invisible, to convince 'em that there is a God, and declare to 'em what manner of being he is, and to convince 'em that he governs and will judge the world, and that there is a future state of rewards and punishments, and to preach to 'em a Christ in heaven and at the right hand of God in an unseen world, shall then meet their people in the most immediate sensible presence of this great God, Saviour and Judge, appearing in the most plain, visible and open manner, with great glory, with all his holy angels, before them and the whole world. They shall not meet them to hear about an absent Christ, an unseen Lord and future Judge; but to appear before that Judge, and as being set together in the presence of that supreme Lord, in his immense glory and awful majesty, whom they have heard so often of in their meetings together on earth.

(4) The meeting, at the last day, of ministers, and the people that have been under their care, will not be attended by any one with a careless, heedless heart.

With such an heart are their meetings often attended in this world by many persons, having little regard to him whom they pretend unitedly to adore in the solemn duties of his public worship, taking little heed to their own thoughts or frame of their minds, not attending to the business they are engaged in, or considering the end for which they are come together. But the meeting at that great day will be very different: there will not be one careless heart, no sleeping, no wandering of mind from the great concern of the meeting, no inattentiveness to the business of the day, no regardlessness of the presence they are in, or of those great things which they shall hear from Christ at that meeting, or that they formerly heard from him and of him by their ministers, in their meeting in a state of trial, or which they shall now hear their ministers declaring concerning them before their judge.

Having observed these things concerning the manner and circumstances of this future meeting of ministers and the people that have been under their care, before the tribunal of Christ at the day of judgment, I now proceed,

II. To observe to what purposes they shall then meet.

1. To give an account, before the great Judge, of their behavior one to another in the relation they stood in to each other in this world.

Ministers are sent forth by Christ to their people on his business, are his servants and messengers; and, when they have finished their service, they must return to their master to give him an account of what they have done, and of the entertainment they have had in performing their ministry. Thus we find, in Luke xiv. 16-21, that when the servant who was sent forth to call the guests to the great supper had done his errand, and finished his appointed service, he returned to his master, and gave him an account of what he had done, and of the entertainment he had received. And when the master, being angry, sent his servant to others, he returns again, and gives his master an account of his conduct and success. So we read, in Heb. xiii. 17, of ministers being rulers in the house of God, "that watch for souls, as those that must give account." And we see by the forementioned Luke xiv., that ministers must give an account to their master, not only of their own behavior in the discharge of their office, but also of their people's reception of them, and of the treatment they have met with among them.

And therefore, as they will be called to give an account of both, they shall give an account at the great day of accounts in the presence of their people; they and their people being both present before their Judge.

Faithful ministers will then give an account with joy, concerning those who have received them well and made a good improvement of their ministry; and these will be given 'em, at that day, as their crown of rejoicing. And, at the same time, they will give an account of the ill treatment of such as have not well received them and their messages from Christ: they will meet these, not as they used to do in this world, to counsel and warn them, but to bear witness against them, and as their judges and assessors with Christ, to condemn them. And on the other hand, the people will, at that day, rise up in judgment against wicked and unfaithful ministers who have sought their own temporal interest more than the good of the souls of their flock.

2. At that time ministers, and the people who have been under their care, shall meet together before Christ, that he may judge between them, as to any controversies which have subsisted between them in this world.

So it very often comes to pass in this evil world, that great differences and controversies arise between ministers and the people that are under their pastoral care. Though they are under the greatest obligations to live in peace, above persons in almost any relation whatever; and although contests and dissensions between persons so related are the most unhappy and terrible in their consequences, on many accounts, of any sort of contentions; yet how frequent have such contentions been! Sometimes a people contest with their ministers about their doctrine, sometimes about their administrations and conduct, and sometimes about their maintenance; and sometimes such contests continue a long time; and sometimes they are decided in this world according to the prevailing interest of one party or the other, rather than by the word of God and the reason of things; and sometimes such controversies never have any proper determination in this world.

But at the day of judgment there will be a full, perfect and everlasting decision of them. The infallible Judge, the infinite fountain of light, truth and justice, will judge between the contending parties, and will declare what is the truth, who is in the right, and what is agreeable to his mind and will. And in order hereto the parties must stand together before him at the last day; which will be the great day of finishing and determining all controversies, rectifying all mistakes and abolishing all unrighteous judgments, errors and confusions, which have before subsisted in the world of mankind.

3. Ministers, and the people that have been under their care, must meet together at that time to receive an eternal sentence and retribution from the judge, in the presence of each other, according to their behavior in the relation they stood in one to another in the present state.

The Judge will not only declare justice, but he will do justice between ministers and their people. He will declare what is right between them, approving him that has been just and faithful, and condemning the unjust; and perfect truth and equity shall take place in the sentence which he passes, in the rewards he bestows and the punishments which he inflicts. There shall be a glorious reward to faithful ministers: to those who have been successful: Dan. xii. 3, "And they that be wise shall shine as the brightness of the firmament; and they that turn many to righteousness as the stars forever and ever;" and also to those who have been faithful, and yet not successful: Isa. xlix. 4, "Then I said, I have labored in vain, I have spent my strength for nought: yet surely my judgment is with the Lord, and my reward with my God." And those who have well received and entertained them shall be gloriously rewarded: Matt. x. 40, 41, "He that receiveth you receiveth me, and he that receiveth me receiveth him that sent me. He that receiveth a prophet in the name of a prophet shall receive a prophet's reward; and he that receiveth a righteous man in the name of a righteous man shall receive a righteous man's reward." Such people, and their faithful ministers, shall be each other's crown of rejoicing: 1 Thess. ii. 19, 20, "For what is our hope, or joy, or crown of rejoicing? Are not even ye in the presence of our Lord Jesus Christ at his coming? For ye are our glory and joy." And in the text, *We are your rejoicing, as ye also are ours, in the day of the Lord Jesus.* But they that evil entreat Christ's faithful ministers, especially in that wherein they are faithful, shall be severely punished: Matt. x. 14, 15, "And whosoever shall not receive you, nor hear your words, when ye depart out of that house or city, shake off the dust of your feet. Verily I say unto you, It shall be more tolerable for the sinners of Sodom and Gomorrah in the day of judgment, than for that city." Deut. xxxiii. 8-11, "And of Levi he said, Let thy Urim and thy Thummim be with thy holy one.... They shall teach Jacob thy judgments, and Israel thy law.... Bless, Lord, his substance, and accept the work of his hands: smite through the loins of them that rise against him, and of them that hate him, that they rise not again." On the other hand, those ministers who are found to have been unfaithful shall have a most terrible punishment. See Ezek. xxxiii. 6; Matt. xxiii. 1-33.

Thus justice shall be administered at the great day to ministers and their people. And to that end they shall meet together, that they may not only receive justice to themselves, but see justice done to the other party: for this is the end of that great day, to reveal or declare the righteous judgment of God, Rom. ii. 5. Ministers shall have justice done them, and they shall see justice done to their people: and the people shall receive justice and see justice done to their minister. And so all things will be adjusted and settled forever between them; every one being sentenced and recompensed according to his works, either in receiving and wearing a crown of eternal joy and glory, or in suffering everlasting shame and pain.

I come now to the next thing proposed, viz.,

III. To give some reasons why we may suppose God has so ordered it, that ministers, and the people that have been under their care, shall meet together at the day of judgment, in such a manner and for such purposes.

There are two things which I would now observe:

1. The mutual concerns of ministers and their people are of the greatest importance.

The Scripture declares, that God will bring every work into judgment with every secret thing, whether it be good or whether it be evil. 'Tis fit that all the concerns and all the behavior of mankind, both public and private, should be brought at last before God's tribunal, and finally determined by an infallible Judge: but it is especially requisite that it should be thus, as to affairs of very great importance.

Now the mutual concerns of a Christian minister and his church and congregation are of the vastest importance: in many respects, of much greater moment than the temporal concerns of the greatest earthly monarchs and their kingdoms or empires. It is of vast consequence how ministers discharge their office, and conduct themselves towards their people in the work of the ministry, and in affairs appertaining to it. 'Tis also a matter of vast importance, how a people receive and entertain a faithful minister of Christ, and what improvement they make of his ministry. These things have a more immediate and direct respect to the great and last end for which man was made, and the eternal welfare of mankind, than any of the temporal concerns of men, whether public or private. And therefore 'tis especially fit that these affairs should be brought into judgment and openly determined and settled in truth and righteousness; and that to this end, ministers and their people should meet together before the omniscient and infallible Judge.

2. The mutual concerns of ministers and their people have a special relation to the main things appertaining to the day of judgment.

They have a special relation to that great and divine person who will then appear as Judge. Ministers are his messengers, sent forth by him; and, in their office and administrations among their people, represent his person, stand in his stead, as those that are sent to declare his mind, to do his work and to speak and act in his name. And therefore 'tis especially fit that they should return to him, to give an account of their work and success. The king is judge of all his subjects, they are all accountable to him. But it is more especially requisite that the king's ministers, who are especially intrusted with the administrations of his kingdom, and that are sent forth on some special negotiation, should return to him, to give an account of themselves, and their discharge of their trust, and the reception they have met with.

Ministers are not only messengers of the person who at the last day will appear as Judge, but the errand they are sent upon, and the affairs they have committed to them as his ministers, do most immediately concern his honor and the interest of his kingdom. The work they are sent upon is to promote the designs of his administration and government; and therefore their business with their people has a near relation to the day of judgment; for the great end of that day is completely to settle and establish the affairs of his kingdom, to adjust all things that pertain to it, that every thing that is opposite to the interests of his kingdom may be removed, and that every thing which contributes to the completeness and glory of it may be perfected and confirmed, that this great King may receive his due honor and glory.

Again, the mutual concerns of ministers and their people have a direct relation to the concerns of the day of judgment, as the business of ministers with their people is to promote the eternal salvation of the souls of men and their escape from eternal damnation; and the day of judgment is the day appointed for that end, openly to decide and settle men's eternal state, to fix some in a state of eternal salvation and to bring their salvation to its utmost consummation, and to fix others in a state of everlasting damnation and most perfect misery. The mutual concerns of ministers and people have a most direct relation to the day of judgment, as the very design of the work of the ministry is the people's preparation for that day. Ministers are sent to warn them of the approach of that day, to forewarn them of the dreadful sentence then to be pronounced on the wicked, and declare to them the blessed sentence then to be pronounced on the righteous, and to use means with them that they may escape the wrath which is then to come on the ungodly, and obtain the reward then to be bestowed on the saints.

And as the mutual concerns of ministers and their people have so near and direct a relation to that day, it is especially fit that those concerns should be brought into that day, and there settled and issued; and that in order to this, ministers and their people should meet and appear together before the great Judge at that day.

APPLICATION

The improvement I would make of the things which have been observed, is to lead the people here present who have been under my pastoral care to some reflections, and give them some advice suitable to our present circumstances; relating to what has been lately done in order to our being separated, as to the relation we have heretofore stood in one to another; but expecting to meet each other before the great tribunal at the day of judgment.

The deep and serious consideration of that our future most solemn meeting is certainly most suitable at such a time as this; there having so lately been that done, which, in all probability, will (as to the relation we have heretofore stood in) be followed with an everlasting separation.

How often have we met together in the house of God in this relation! How often have I spoke to you, instructed, counselled, warned, directed and fed you, and administered ordinances among you, as the people which were committed to my care, and whose precious souls I had the charge of! But in all probability this never will be again.°

The prophet Jeremiah (chap. xxv. 3), puts the people in mind how long he had labored among them in the work of the ministry: "From the thirteenth year of Josiah the son of Amon king of Judah, even unto this day, that is the three and twentieth year, the word of the Lord came unto me, and I have spoken unto you, rising early and speaking." I am not about to compare myself with the prophet Jeremiah; but in this respect I can say as he did, that "I have spoken the word of God to you unto the three and twentieth year, rising early and speaking." It was three and twenty years, the 15th day of last February, since I have labored in the work of the ministry, in the relation of a pastor to this church and congregation. And though my strength has been weakness, having always labored under great infirmity of body, besides my insufficiency for so great a charge in other respects, yet I have not spared my feeble strength, but have exerted it for the good of your souls. I can appeal to you as the apostle does to his bearers, Gal. iv. 13, "Ye know how through infirmity of the flesh I preached the gospel unto you." I have spent the prime of my life and strength in labors for your eternal welfare. You are my witnesses, that what strength I have had I have not neglected in idleness, nor laid out in prosecuting worldly schemes and managing temporal affairs, for the advancement of my outward estate, and aggrandizing myself and family; but have given myself wholly to the work of the ministry, laboring in it night and day, rising early and applying myself to this great business to which Christ appointed me. I have found the work of the ministry among you to be a great work indeed, a work of exceeding care, labor and difficulty: many have been the heavy burdens that I have borne in it, which my strength has been very unequal to. God called me to bear these burdens; and I bless his name, that he has so supported me as to keep me from sinking under them, and that his power herein has been manifested in my weakness; so that although I have often been troubled on every side, yet I have not been distressed; perplexed, but not in despair; cast down, but not destroyed.

But now I have reason to think my work is finished which I had to do as your minister: you have publicly rejected me, and my opportunities cease.

How highly therefore does it now become us to consider of that time when we must meet one another before the chief Shepherd! When I must give an account of my stewardship, of the service I have done for, and the reception and treatment I have had among, the people he sent me to: and you must give an account of your own conduct towards me, and the improvement you have made of these three and twenty years of my ministry. For then both you and I must appear together, and we both must give an account, in order to an infallible, righteous and eternal sentence to be passed upon us by him who will judge us with respect to all that we have said or done in our meeting here, all our conduct one towards another, in the house of God and elsewhere, on Sabbath days and on other days; who will try our hearts and manifest our thoughts, and the principles and frames of our minds, will judge us with respect to all the controversies which have subsisted between us, with the strictest impartiality, and will examine our treatment of each other in those controversies. There is nothing covered that shall not be revealed, nor hid which shall not be known; all will be examined in the searching, penetrating light of God's omniscience and glory, and by him whose eyes are as a flame of fire; and truth and right shall be made plainly to appear, being stripped of every veil; and all error, falsehood, unrighteousness and injury shall be laid open, stripped of every disguise; every specious pretence, every cavil and all false reasoning shall vanish in a moment, as not being able to bear the light of that day. And then our hearts will be turned inside out, and the secrets of them will be made more plainly to appear than our outward actions do now. Then it shall appear what the ends are which we have aimed at, what have been the governing principles which we have acted from, and what have been the dispositions we have exercised in our ecclesiastical disputes and contests. Then it will appear whether I acted uprightly, and from a truly conscientious, careful regard to my duty to my great Lord and Master, in some former ecclesiastical controversies, which have been attended with exceeding unhappy circumstances and consequences: it will appear whether there was any just cause for the resentment which was manifested on those occasions. And then our late grand controversy, concerning the qualifications necessary for admission to the privileges of members in complete standing in the visible church of Christ, will be examined and judged in all its parts and circumstances, and the whole set forth in a clear, certain and perfect light. Then it will appear whether the doctrine which I have preached and published concerning this matter be Christ's own doctrine, whether he will not own it as one of the precious truths which have proceeded from his own mouth, and vindicate and honor as such before the whole universe. Then it will appear what is meant by "the man that comes without the wedding garment"; for that is the day spoken of, Matt. xxii. 13, wherein such an one shall be bound hand and foot, and cast into outer darkness, where shall be weeping and gnashing of teeth. And then it will appear whether, in declaring this doctrine, and acting agreeable to it, and in my general conduct in the affair, I have been influenced from any regard to my own temporal interest or honor, or desire to appear wiser than others; or have acted from any sinister, secular views whatsoever; and whether what I have done has not been from a careful, strict and tender regard to the will of my Lord and Master, and because I dare not offend him, being satisfied what his will was, after a long, diligent, impartial and prayerful inquiry; having this constantly in view and prospect to engage me to great solicitude not rashly to determine truth to be on this side of the question, where I am now persuaded it is, that such a determination would not be for my temporal interest, but every way against it, bringing a long series of extreme difficulties and plunging me into an abyss of trouble and sorrow. And then it will appear whether my people have done their duty to their pastor with respect to this matter; whether they have shown a right temper and spirit on this occasion; whether they have done me justice in hearing, attending to and considering what I had to say in evidence of what I believed and taught as part of the counsel of God; whether I have been treated with that impartiality, candor and regard which the just Judge esteemed due; and whether, in the many steps which have been taken and the many things that have been said and done in the course of this controversy, righteousness and charity and Christian decorum have been maintained; or, if otherwise, to how great a degree these things have been violated. Then every step of the conduct of each of us in this affair, from first to last, and the spirit we have exercised in all shall be examined and manifested, and our own consciences shall speak plain and loud, and each of us shall be convinced, and the world shall know; and never shall there be any more mistake, misrepresentation or misapprehension of the affair to eternity.

This controversy is now probably brought to an issue between you and me as to this world; it has issued in the event of the week before last: but it must have another decision at that great day, which certainly will come, when you and I shall meet together before the great judgment seat: and therefore I leave it to that time, and shall say no more about it at present.

But I would now proceed to address myself particularly to several sorts of persons.

I. To those who are professors of godliness amongst us.

I would now call you to a serious consideration of that great day wherein you must meet him who has heretofore been your pastor, before the Judge whose eyes are as a flame of fire.

I have endeavored, according to my best ability, to search the word of God, with regard to the distinguishing notes of true piety, those by which persons might best discover their state, and most surely and clearly judge of themselves. And these rules and marks I have from time to time applied to you in the preaching of the word to the utmost of my skill, and in the most plain and searching manner that I have been able, in order to the detecting the deceived hypocrite and establishing the hopes and comforts of the sincere. And yet 'tis to be feared, that after all that I have done, I now leave some of you in a deceived, deluded state; for 'tis not to be supposed that among several hundred professors, none are deceived.

Henceforward I am like to have no more opportunity to take the care and charge of your souls, to examine and search them. But still I entreat you to remember and consider the rules which I have often laid down to you during my ministry, with a solemn regard to the future day when you and I must meet together before our Judge; when the uses of examination you have heard from me must be rehearsed again before you, and those rules of trial must be tried, and it will appear whether they have been good or not; and it will also appear whether you have impartially heard them, and tried yourselves by them; and the Judge himself, who is infallible, will try both you and me: and after this none will be deceived concerning the state of their souls.

I have often put you in mind that, whatever your pretences to experiences, discoveries, comforts and joys have been, at that day every one will be judged according to his works; and then you will find it so.

May you have a minister of greater knowledge of the word of God and better acquaintance with soul cases, and of greater skill in applying himself to souls, whose discourses may be more searching and convincing; that such of you as have held fast deceit under my preaching may have your eyes opened by his; that you may be undeceived before that great day.

What means and helps for instruction and self-examination you may hereafter have is uncertain; but one thing is certain, that the time is short, your opportunity for rectifying mistakes in so important a concern will soon come to an end. We live in a world of great changes. There is now a great change come to pass; you have withdrawn yourselves from my ministry under which you have continued for so many years: but the time is coming, and will soon come, when you will pass out of time into eternity; and so will pass from under all means of grace whatsoever.

The greater part of you who are professors of godliness have (to use the phrase of the apostle) "acknowledged me in part": you have heretofore acknowledged me to be your spiritual father, the instrument of the greatest good to you that ever is or can be obtained by any of the children of men. Consider of that day when you and I shall meet before our Judge, when it shall be examined whether you have had from me the treatment which is due to spiritual children, and whether you have treated me as you ought to have treated a spiritual father. As the relation of a natural parent brings great obligations on children in the sight of God; so much more, in many respects, does the relation of a spiritual father bring great obligations on such whose conversation and eternal salvation they suppose God has made them the instrument of: 1 Cor. iv. 15. "For though you have ten thousand instructors in Christ, yet have ye not many fathers: for in Christ Jesus I have begotten you through the gospel."

II. Now I am taking my leave of this people I would apply myself to such among them as I leave in a Christless, graceless condition; and would call on such seriously to consider of that solemn day when they and I must meet before the Judge of the world.

My parting with you is in some respects in a peculiar manner a melancholy parting; inasmuch as I leave you in most melancholy circumstances; because I leave you in the gall of bitterness and bond of iniquity, having the wrath of God abiding on you, and remaining under condemnation to everlasting misery and destruction. Seeing I must leave you, it would have been a comfortable and happy circumstance of our parting if I had left you in Christ, safe and blessed in that sure refuge and glorious rest of the saints. But it is otherwise. I leave you far off, aliens and strangers, wretched subjects and captives of sin and Satan and prisoners of vindictive justice; without Christ and without God in the world.

Your consciences bear me witness, that while I had opportunity, I have not ceased to warn you and set before you your danger. I have studied to represent the misery and necessity of your circumstances in the clearest manner possible. I have tried all ways that I could think of tending to awaken your consciences, and make you sensible of the necessity of your improving your time, and being speedy in flying from the wrath to come and thorough in the use of means for your escape and safety. I have diligently endeavored to find out and use the most powerful motives to persuade you to take care for your own welfare and salvation. I have not only endeavored to awaken you, that you might be moved with fear, but I have used my utmost endeavors to win you: I have sought out acceptable words, that if possible I might prevail upon you to forsake sin, and turn to God, and accept of Christ as your Saviour and Lord. I have spent my strength very much in these things. But yet, with regard to you whom I am now speaking to, I have not been successful: but have this day reason to complain in those words, Jer. vi. 29: "The bellows are burnt, the lead is consumed of the fire; the founder melteth in vain: for the wicked are not plucked away." 'Tis to be feared that all my labors, as to many of you, have served no other purpose but to harden you; and that the word which I have preached, instead of being a savor of life unto life, has been a savor of death unto death. Though I shall not have any account to give for the future of such as have openly and resolutely renounced my ministry, as of a betrustment committed to me: yet remember you must give account for yourselves of your care of your own souls, and your improvement of all means past and future, through your whole lives. God only knows what will become of your poor, perishing souls, what means you may hereafter enjoy, or what disadvantages and temptations you may be under. May God in his mercy grant that, however all past means have been unsuccessful, you may have future means which may have a new effect; and that the word of God, as it shall be hereafter dispensed to you, may prove as the fire and the hammer that breaketh the rock in pieces. However, let me now at parting exhort and beseech you not wholly to forget the warnings you have had while under my ministry. When you and I shall meet at the day of judgment, then you will remember 'em: the sight of me, your former minister, on that occasion, will soon revive 'em in your memory; and that in a very affecting manner. O don't let that be the first time that they are so revived.

You and I are now parting one from another as to this world; let us labor that we mayn't be parted after our meeting at the last day. If I have been your faithful pastor (which will that day appear, whether I have or no), then I shall be acquitted, and shall ascend with Christ. O do your part, that in such a case it may not be so, that you should be forced eternally to part from me and all that have been faithful in Christ Jesus. This is a sorrowful parting that now is between you and me, but that would be a more sorrowful parting to you than this. This you may perhaps bear without being much affected with it, if you are not glad of it; but such a parting in that day will most deeply, sensibly and dreadfully affect you.

III. I would address myself to those who are under some awakenings.

Blessed be God that there are some such, and that (although I have reason to fear I leave multitudes in this large congregation in a Christless state) yet I do not leave them all in total stupidity and carelessness about their souls. Some of you that I have reason to hope are under some awakenings, have acquainted me with your circumstances; which has a tendency to cause me, now I am leaving you, to take my leave of you with peculiar concern for you. What will be the issue of your present exercise of mind I know not: but it will be known at that day, when you and I shall meet before the judgment seat of Christ. Therefore now be much in consideration of that day.

Now I am parting with this flock, I would once more press upon you the counsels I have heretofore given, to take heed of being slighty in so great a concern, to be thorough and in good earnest in the affair, and to beware of backsliding, to hold on and hold out to the end. And cry mightily to God, that these great changes that pass over this church and congregation don't prove your overthrow. There is great temptation in them; and the devil will undoubtedly seek to make his advantage of them, if possible to cause your present convictions and endeavors to be abortive. You had need to double your diligence, and watch and pray, lest you be overcome by temptation.

Whoever may hereafter stand related to you as your spiritual guide, my desire and prayer is, that the great Shepherd of the sheep would have a special respect to you, and be your guide (for there is none teacheth like him), and that he who is the infinite fountain of light would "open your eyes, and turn you from darkness unto light, and from the power of Satan unto God; that you may receive forgiveness of sins, and inheritance among them that are sanctified, through faith that is in Christ;" that so, in that great day, when I shall meet you again before your Judge and mine, we may meet in joyful and glorious circumstances, never to be separated any more.

IV. I would apply myself to the young people of the congregation.

Since I have been settled in the work of the ministry in this place I have ever had a peculiar concern for the souls of the young people, and a desire that religion might flourish among them: and have especially exerted myself in order to it; because I knew the special opportunity they had beyond others, and that ordinarily those whom God intended mercy for, were brought to fear and love him in their youth. And it has ever appeared to me a peculiarly amiable thing, to see young people walking in the ways of virtue and Christian piety, having their hearts purified and sweetened with a principle of divine love. And it has appeared a thing exceeding beautiful, and what would be much to the adorning and happiness of the town, if the young people could be persuaded when they meet together, to converse as Christians, and as the children of God; avoiding impurity, levity and extravagance; keeping strictly to the rules of virtue, and conversing together of the things of God and Christ and heaven. This is what I have longed for: and it has been exceeding grievous to me when I have heard of vice, vanity and disorder among our youth. And so far as I know my own heart, it was from hence that I formerly led this church to some measures for the suppressing of vice among our young people, which gave so great offence, and by which I became so obnoxious.° I have sought the good, and not the hurt of our young people. I have desired their truest honor and happiness, and not their reproach; knowing that true virtue and religion tended not only to the glory and felicity of young people in another world, but their greatest peace and prosperity, and highest dignity and honor, in this world; and above all things to sweeten and render pleasant and delightful even the days of youth.

But whether I have loved you and sought your good more or less, yet God in his providence now calling me to part with you, committing your souls to him who once committed the pastoral care of them to me, nothing remains but only (as I am now taking my leave of you) earnestly to beseech you, from love to yourselves, if you have none to me, not to despise and forget the warnings and counsels I have so often given you; remembering the day when you and I must meet again before the great Judge of quick and dead; when it will appear whether the things I have taught you were true, whether the counsels I have given you were good, and whether I truly sought your good, and whether you have well improved my endeavors.

I have, from time to time, earnestly warned you against frolicking (as it is called), and some other liberties commonly taken by young people in the land. And whatever some may say in justification of such liberties and customs, and may laugh at warnings against them, I now leave you my parting testimony against such things; not doubting but God will approve and confirm it in that day when we shall meet before him.°

V. I would apply myself to the children of the congregation, the lambs of this flock, who have been so long under my care.

I have just now said that I have had a peculiar concern for the young people; and in so saying I did not intend to exclude you. You are in youth, and in the most early youth: and therefore I have been sensible that if those that were young had a precious opportunity for their souls' good, you who are very young had, in many respects, a peculiarly precious opportunity. And accordingly I have not neglected you: I have endeavored to do the part of a faithful shepherd, in feeding the lambs as well as the sheep. Christ did once commit the care of your souls to me as your minister; and you know, dear children, how I have instructed you, and warned you from time to time; you know how I have often called you together for that end; and some of you, sometimes, have seemed to be affected with what I have said to you. But I am afraid it has had no saving effects as to many of you; but that you remain still in an unconverted condition, without any real saving work wrought in your souls, convincing you thoroughly of your sin and misery, causing you to see the great evil of sin, and to mourn for it, and hate it above all things, and giving you a sense of the excellency of the Lord Jesus Christ, bringing you with all your hearts to cleave to him as your Saviour, weaning your hearts from the world, and causing you to love God above all, and to delight in holiness more than in all the pleasant things of this earth; and so that I now leave you in a miserable condition, having no interest in Christ, and so under the awful displeasure and anger of God, and in danger of going down to the pit of eternal misery.

But now I must bid you farewell: I must leave you in the hands of God; I can do no more for you than to pray for you. Only I desire you not to forget, but often think of the counsels and warnings I have given you, and the endeavors I have used, that your souls might be saved from everlasting destruction.

Dear children, I leave you in an evil world, that is full of snares and temptations. God only knows what will become of you. This the Scripture hath told us, that there are but few saved; and we have abundant confirmation of it from what we see. This we see, that children die as well as others: multitudes die before they grow up; and of those that grow up, comparatively few ever give good evidence of saving conversion to God. I pray God to pity you, and take care of you, and provide for you the best means for the good of your souls; and that God himself would undertake for you to be your heavenly Father and the mighty Redeemer of your immortal souls. Do not neglect to pray for yourselves: take heed you ben't of the number of those who cast off fear and restrain prayer before God. Constantly pray to God in secret; and often remember that great day when you must appear before the judgment seat of Christ, and meet your minister there, who has so often counselled and warned you.

I conclude with a few words of advice to all in general, in some particulars, which are of great importance in order to the welfare and prosperity of this church and congregation.

1. One thing that greatly concerns you, as you would be a happy people, is the maintaining of family order.

We have had great disputes how the church ought to be regulated; and indeed the subject of these disputes was of great importance: but the due regulation of your families is of no less, and, in some respects, of much greater importance. Every Christian family ought to be as it were a little church, consecrated to Christ, and wholly influenced and governed by his rules. And family education and order are some of the chief of the means of grace. If these fail, all other means are like to prove ineffectual. If these are duly maintained, all the means of grace will be like to prosper and be successful.

Let me now, therefore, once more, before I finally cease to speak to this congregation, repeat and earnestly press the counsel which I have often urged on heads of families here, while I was their pastor, to great painfulness in teaching, warning and directing their children; bringing them up in the nurture and admonition of the Lord; beginning early, where there is yet opportunity, and maintaining a constant diligence in labors of this kind; remembering that, as you would not have all your instructions and counsels ineffectual, there must be government as well as instructions, which must be maintained with an even hand and steady resolution, as a guard to the religion and morals of the family and the support of its good order. Take heed that it be not with any of you as with Eli of old, who reproved his children but restrained them not; and that, by this means, you don't bring the like curse on your families as he did on his.

And let children obey their parents, and yield to their instructions, and submit to their orders, as they would inherit a blessing and not a curse. For we have reason to think, from many things in the word of God, that nothing has a greater tendency to bring a curse on persons in this world, and on all their temporal concerns, than an undutiful, unsubmissive, disorderly behavior in children towards their parents.

2. As you would seek the future prosperity of this society, it is of vast importance that you should avoid contention.

A contentious people will be a miserable people. The contentions which have been among you, since I first became your pastor, have been one of the greatest burdens I have labored under in the course of my ministry: not only the contentions you have had with me, but those which you have had one with another about your lands and other concerns: because I knew that contention, heat of spirit, evil speaking, and things of the like nature, were directly contrary to the spirit of Christianity, and did, in a peculiar manner, tend to drive away God's Spirit from a people and to render all means of grace ineffectual, as well as to destroy a people's outward comfort and welfare.

Let me therefore earnestly exhort you, as you would seek your own future good hereafter, to watch against a contentious spirit.° If you would see good days, seek peace, and ensue it, 1 Pet. iii. 10, 11. Let the contention which has lately been about the terms of Christian communion, as it has been the greatest of your contentions, so be the last of them. I would, now I am preaching my farewell sermon, say to you, as the Apostle to the Corinthians, 2 Cor. xiii. 11, 12: "Finally, brethren, farewell. Be perfect, be of one mind, live in peace; and the God of love and peace shall be with you."

And here I would particularly advise those that have adhered to me in the late controversy, to watch over their spirits and avoid all bitterness towards others. Your temptations are, in some respects, the greatest; because what has been lately done is grievous to you. But however wrong you may think others have done, maintain, with great diligence and watchfulness, a Christian meekness and sedateness of spirit; and labor, in this respect, to excel others who are of the contrary part. And this will be the best victory: for "he that rules his spirit, is better than he that takes a city." Therefore let nothing be done through strife or vainglory. Indulge no revengeful spirit in any wise; but watch and pray against it; and, by all means in your power, seek the prosperity of the town: and never think you behave yourselves as becomes Christians, but when you sincerely, sensibly and fervently love all men, of whatever party or opinion, and whether friendly or unkind, just or injurious, to you or your friends, or to the cause and kingdom of Christ.

3. Another thing that vastly concerns the future prosperity of this town, is, that you should watch against the encroachments of error; and particularly Arminianism and doctrines of like tendency. You were, many of you, as I well remember, much alarmed with the apprehension of the danger of the prevailing of these corrupt principles near sixteen years ago. But the danger then was small in comparison of what appears now. These doctrines at this day are much more prevalent than they were then: the progress they have made in the land, within this seven years, seems to have been vastly greater than at any time in the like space before: and they are still prevailing and creeping into almost all parts of the land, threatening the utter ruin of the credit of those doctrines which are the peculiar glory of the gospel, and the interests of vital piety. And I have of late perceived some things among yourselves that show that you are far from being out of danger, but on the contrary remarkably exposed. The older people may perhaps think themselves sufficiently fortified against infection; but it is fit that all should beware of self-confidence and carnal security, and should remember those needful warnings of sacred writ, "Be not high-minded, but fear;" and "let him that stands, take heed lest he fall." But let the case of the older people be as it will, the rising generation are doubtless greatly exposed. These principles are exceeding taking with corrupt nature, and are what young people, at least such as have not their hearts established with grace, are easily led away with. And if these principles should greatly prevail in this town, as they very lately have done in another large town I could name, formerly greatly noted for religion, and so for a long time, it will threaten the spiritual and eternal ruin of this people in the present and future generations. Therefore you have need of the greatest and most diligent care and watchfulness with respect to this matter.

4. Another thing which I would advise to, that you may hereafter be a prosperous people, is, that you would give yourselves much to prayer. God is the fountain of all blessing and prosperity, and he will be sought to for his blessing. I would therefore advise you not only to be constant in secret and family prayer, and in the public worship of God in his house, but also often to assemble yourselves in private praying societies. I would advise all such as are grieved for the afflictions of Joseph, and sensibly affected with the calamities of this town, of whatever opinion they be with relation to the subject of our late controversy, often to meet together for prayer, and to cry to God for his mercy to themselves, and mercy to this town, and mercy to Zion and the people of God in general through the world.

5. The last article of advice I would give (which doubtless does greatly concern your prosperity), is, that you would take great care with regard to the settlement of a minister, to see to it who, or what manner of person he is that you settle; and particularly in these two respects:

(1) That he be a man of thoroughly sound principles in the scheme of doctrine which he maintains.

This you will stand in the greatest need of, especially at such a day of corruption as this is. And in order to obtain such a one, you had need to exercise extraordinary care and prudence. I know the danger. I know the manner of many young gentlemen of corrupt principles, their ways of concealing themselves, the fair, specious disguises they are wont to put on, by which they deceive others, to maintain their own credit, and get themselves into others' confidence and improvement, and secure and establish their own interest, until they see a convenient opportunity to begin more openly to broach and propagate their corrupt tenets.

(2) Labor to obtain a man who has an established character, as a person of serious religion and fervent piety.

It is of vast importance that those who are settled in this work should be men of true piety, at all times, and in all places; but more especially at some times, and in some towns and churches. And this present time, which is a time wherein religion is in danger, by so many corruptions in doctrine and practice, is in a peculiar manner a day wherein such ministers are necessary. Nothing else but sincere piety of heart is at all to be depended on, at such a time as this, as a security to a young man, just coming into the world, from the prevailing infection, or thoroughly to engage him in proper and successful endeavors to withstand and oppose the torrent of error and prejudice against the high, mysterious, evangelical doctrines of the religion of Jesus Christ, and their genuine effects in true experimental religion. And this place is a place that does peculiarly need such a minister, for reasons obvious to all.If you should happen to settle a minister who knows nothing truly of Christ and the way of salvation by him, nothing experimentally of the nature of vital religion; alas, how will you be exposed as sheep without a shepherd! Here is need of one in this place, who shall be eminently fit to stand in the gap and make up the hedge, and who shall be as the chariots of Israel and the horsemen thereof. You need one that shall stand as a champion in the cause of truth and the power of godliness.

Having briefly mentioned these important articles of advice, nothing remains but that I now take my leave of you, and bid you all *farewell*, wishing and praying for your best prosperity. I would now commend your immortal souls to him, who formerly committed them to me, expecting the day, when I must meet you again before him, who is the Judge of quick and dead. I desire that I may never forget this people, who have been so long my special charge, and that I may never cease fervently to pray for your prosperity. May God bless you with a faithful pastor, one that is well acquainted with his mind and will, thoroughly warning sinners, wisely and skilfully searching professors, and conducting you in the way to eternal blessedness. May you have truly a burning and shining light set up in this candlestick; and may you, not only for a season, but during his whole life, and that a long life, be willing to rejoice in his light. And let me be remembered in the prayers of all God's people that are of a calm spirit, and are peaceable and faithful in Israel, of whatever opinion they may be with respect to terms of church communion. And let us all remember and never forget our future solemn meeting on that great day of the Lord; the day of infallible decision and of the everlasting and unalterable sentence. AMEN.

Made in the USA
Lexington, KY
30 November 2015